Give feedback on the book at:
lorhainneeckhart@hotmail.com

Twitter: @LEckhart
Facebook: AuthorLorhainneEckhart

Printed in the U.S.A

One Night

KATE & WALKER

BOOK ONE

LORHAINNE ECKHART

New York Times & USA Today Bestselling Author Lorhainne Eckhart brings you ONE NIGHT, A high-stakes suspense and sizzling, red-hot romance!

A blind date goes deadly on a night she'll never forget!

Kate Sikes has it all: she's smart and sexy, she has a great career, and she really does believe in happy endings—only she always picks the wrong guys. Nonetheless, she's determined to meet the man of her dreams, and she believes she's finally found the one when she turns to online dating. However, her high hopes are once again dashed when Mr. Right turns out to be Mr. Wrong, with some seriously heavy baggage that has Kate running for her life.

When Detective Walker Pruett comes to Kate's rescue not once but twice, he realizes the only way to keep her safe from a crazy stalker is to keep her close. But his life is far from easy. He's a lone wolf, and the last thing he's looking for is attachment. After One Night with Kate, though, Walker can't fight the chemistry sizzling between them. Not only does he find her irresistible, he feels compelled to protect her.

And Kate soon discovers just how far Walker will go to do so.

CHAPTER

One

Kate Sikes's short-lived online dating venture started with a MacBook Pro, a pair of killer heels, and a trip to the salon. How it ended was deadly.

For nearly her entire young adult life—she was now at the ripe old age of twenty-two—Kate had continually dated the wrong guys, losers looking to freeload off her success. She'd remained hopeful even though each guy she fell for lacked ambition. When she met the last guy, Todd, she'd been convinced her luck had changed, as he was an up and coming stockbroker whose one and only fault was that he lived with his mother. However, she soon discovered that Todd had anxiety issues and preferred to consult his mother before making any plans. So Kate, in one of her smarter decisions, had said goodbye.

Kate Sikes was the assistant front desk manager at the Hotel Monaco. She was smart, attractive, a hard worker, and on track for manager. She lacked nothing in her career. She was ambitious, a self-starter, and had the ability to think outside the box—at least according to her last evaluation. Kate decided that whatever kept attracting her to the same passive-aggressive, noncommittal losers was about to change. That big old "S" for "stupid" tattooed to her forehead was going to be erased. She was turning over a new leaf, reevaluating herself, and determined to find a suitable match.

So she signed up for one of the premier dating sites, submitted her credit card information, and completed her profile—all accurate, except for her weight. Although she was curvy, not overweight, she decided it was best to keep that last detail to herself. Then she started shopping through profiles. It was like being in a candy story, looking for a match among all those drop-dead gorgeous guys. She waited for a response from all the matches flooding her inbox, weeding out the ones that sounded too good to be true, and voila. It was like hitting the lottery of man-candy heaven.

But not only did she soon discover this wasn't as easy as it had sounded in the dating site's ads, she also found that most men were as noncommittal as the losers she'd been dating—until match number twenty-five: Ryder Connelly, five foot ten, athletic, dark haired, with a smile to die for. He was a dentist who worked out regularly and wanted to meet her. Oh my God! Kate was both excited and a basket of nerves as she finished her shift at the four-star resort. She'd watched the clock all after-noon, knowing she had to be out the door as soon as her shift ended. That left her three hours until she needed to be at the restaurant to meet Ryder and kick off a night of many firsts.

"Taking off for the night, Keith," she told her boss, tapping the frame of the door to the back office.

A short, compact middle-aged man typing away on the computer glanced up. "Have a good night, Kate," he said, leaning back in his ergonomic chair. The hinges squeaked. He twirled a pen between his fingers as he glanced up to her. "Listen, did you handle that room service complaint?"

"I did. Comped them a free dinner in the dining room. The wife was happy. I don't think anything will make the husband happy, though. He was more interested in rehashing how the kitchen put onions on his burger even though he's deathly allergic to them. The wife did tell me he's not really allergic to the onions, he just hates them. At least Jerome is the head waiter tonight. He'll make sure they're given the best. If not…" She waved her hand and stopped talking as Keith shot her an unreadable glance, the same one he always did when he was about to cut her down for something. She hated when he did that, making her feel inadequate.

"I'll follow up, make sure it's handled. Just don't be too liberal with all the freebies you're handing out."

She wanted to roll her eyes. What did Keith expect? He wanted the guests happy but implied that the front desk, at times, should work with nothing. She was about to ask what he would have done to appease the disgruntled couple—who were two of the most frequent reviewers on Trip Advisor—but then decided it was best to drop it before he could question her about something else she'd handled or, worse, suddenly rope her into picking up another shift. Keith was famous for that. So she slipped out the door, telling herself to let it go.

She glanced at her watch as she raced outside onto the concrete sidewalk and next door to the hotel spa, where she'd booked a hair appointment. Theirs was one of the better salons in town, and considering she got a reasonable employee discount, it was a safe bet. She'd considered all afternoon what to do with her hair. She'd added highlights a month ago, but she needed a trim, maybe something different that would frame her round face and bring out her hazel eyes. Her hair was thick, a mousy brown highlighted with blond.

"Hey there, Kate," Darlene said. "Right on time! Come on back to the sink."

Darlene, one of the beauty advisors, was the junior hairdresser on staff. She was tall and slim, close to Kate's age. Because she was a junior, she was half the price but still good—one of the better ones, as far as Kate was concerned. Kate hung up her black blazer on the coat tree in the corner. She smoothed down her staff uniform, a black skirt and white shirt, and followed Darlene to the sink in back.

"Any ideas of what you'd like?" Darlene asked as she scrubbed Kate's hair with shampoo.

"Well, I need a trim for sure. Trying to look my best for tonight. I have a date." She couldn't help the grin pulling at her lips.

"Oh, do tell. Who's the man?"

"He's someone I met online. We've talked some by email and once on the phone, but tonight's the night I get to meet him," she nearly squealed.

"Well, good for you, girl. Let's see what I can do. Are you looking to go shorter or just clean up the style you already have? I've got to tell you, you have great hair." Darlene wrapped a towel around Kate's head and led her to a chair, then pumped it up as she dried the ends of her hair with the towel.

"I don't want to go too short," Kate said. No, she liked that her hair wasn't too long, just past her shoulders. Long enough she could pin it up and short enough it was still manageable. It was thick and had body.

Darlene combed her wet hair and seemed to study it for a minute. "Well, I could layer it a bit to give it more body. That will frame your face nicely, bring out those to-die-for cheeks you have. Do you want me to style it for you too? That will cost extra."

"I planned for it, all the extras, so make me look good," Kate said.

"You got it. By the time I'm through with you, this guy is going to be drooling across the table."

True to her word, Darlene had Kate out of there in under an hour, her hair cut, styled, and shaped, looking better than she could have ever done herself. That left her two hours until she had to meet Ryder at 525, the new hot and trendy restaurant everyone was talking about.

Kate hustled the seven blocks to her building in downtown Portland, to her small one-bedroom apartment on the fifth floor. She bathed, careful not to get her hair wet, and then took her time applying her makeup— not too heavy but enough to give her eyes that smoky, sultry look. Satisfied, she pulled on a red sheath with cap sleeves. It hugged her curves and was low enough that it showed her generous C-cup cleavage. She checked her image in the mirror, turning sideways to see if her control-top hose were working.

Damn, if she didn't look good. Her butt was round and firm, and there was plenty there to hold on to without being too much. She put in a pair of simple gold hoops and slipped on her black stilettos, then stood on a chair in front of the mirror to see if they worked. Damn straight they did, and then some. Fuck-me heels for sure. For a minute, she worried about whether they would send the wrong message. She glanced into her closet, spying her brown wedge heels, which were two inches shorter, manageable, and easier to walk in but did nothing for her legs.

"Stop questioning everything. You look fantastic," she said to herself as she climbed down and then glanced at the clock to see that it was nearly six thirty. Time to go. One last stop on her MacBook Pro. She checked her email and then looked at Ryder's photo from his profile page, memorizing the dimples and the killer smile. Damn, he was good looking. Then she grabbed her keys, her black clutch purse, and her black and white coat and hurried out the door. She heard it click shut behind her, already locked. That was handy, but she worried that if she wasn't careful, she could lock herself out.

Instead of walking the four blocks, which she could easily have done in flats, she hailed a cab and arrived ten minutes early. In front of the busy restaurant, alive with chatter, suits, and all the downtown action, she paid the cabbie and climbed out. The restaurant had a crowded bar on one side and a busy dining room on the other. It was simple, all glass, open concept, with clean lines. The waiters dressed in white and black, serving the best of the best. When Kate pulled open the door and stepped inside, she looked at all the faces filling the waiting area —and then her heel caught on something, and she went down.

She landed on her knees, letting out a squeak. Her palms scraped the carpet, her ass in the air.

"Are you okay?" A man touched her arm, and his grip firmed as he helped her up.

He had a welcome strength, as her legs were shaking and she wasn't sure she could get up on her own, especially in her godawful heels, which were starting to hurt. She could feel her face warming—no, burning—and the sting of where she'd landed on her knees. She glanced into the faces around her: people waiting, staring, watching. She was sure someone was laughing, and of course she was embarrassed as she struggled to remain upright on the stilts she was wearing.

"Yeah, fine, thank you," she said.

She could see into his green eyes. Nice, she'd never seen a man with green eyes before. He had short red hair, not bright or orange but a lighter color. He also had one of those light beards guys got after not shaving for a week. On some guys it looked messy, but on this guy it looked hot. Kate realized he still had her arm and he had a look in his eyes that bordered on appreciation, humor, or maybe annoyance. As he took in her dress and shoes, by the way his eyes lingered, she had a feeling this was a man who didn't apologize for anything.

"Hey, you must be Kate," said a man behind her.

She was startled when the face in the picture she'd memorized appeared beside her. He had the same killer smile with dimples. In person, he was even better looking and could have replaced any of those guys on the cover of *GQ.*

"Ryder!" she said quite exuberantly, attracting more glances. She wanted to kick herself and tone it down a bit.

"Hey, it's a nice to see you," she added, a little softer, feeling about as awkward as she had on her first day of school. At the same time, she wondered whether he'd seen her ass on the floor after her ungraceful entrance. She plastered a practiced smile to her face, the one she used when she was working. When she tried to glance over to the handsome stranger who had helped her up, he was gone.

CHAPTER

Two

"So you're a dentist?" she asked.

What was it about meeting someone for the first time and having to figure out what to say that was so damn hard? For some it was easy, that art of directing a conversation. Then there were those who'd only mastered the art of talking about themselves. She'd dated many of those, the type of guy that made her feel so comfortable that, for a minute, she wanted to trust them with anything and everything, to open up and tell them her biggest, darkest secrets. Big mistake.

It hit her why she was wound so tightly, sitting there in that trendy restaurant, combing her brain, trying her damnedest to think of something intelligent to say: because Ryder was not the typical guy she dated. He was different, and she was determined to remain hopeful that he was, in fact, the real deal.

He flashed her that spectacular dimpled grin, showing off a perfect set of straight white teeth. Of course, being a dentist, he'd had his own teeth fixed, because no one could naturally have been born with such a perfect set of teeth. He held up his hand as he steered the conversation. "I need to clear up a few things first. Just so you know, I'm thirty-five, not twenty-eight. Don't like to put all my personal information on the Internet. You know, hackers."

He had a deep voice. Normally, she loved a man's deep voice, but Ryder's lacked something. It seemed so practiced and unauthentic. Maybe it was just guilt in his voice from lying about his age, or maybe she was getting surface talk without anything genuine. She considered what he'd said, doing the math in her head. She liked older, but thirty-five? That was thirteen years on her. Then again, he did look good—but there was a big difference between five years and thirteen years, considering women lived, on average, longer than men. Her technical mind kicked in. When she'd be in her prime, he'd be an old man.

"Wow, I just can't get over how gorgeous you are." He gestured at her from across the cozy table for two in the corner by the window. It was a nice spot, and she wondered how he'd managed to snag it, considering the wait list for tables in this restaurant was weeks, if not months, long.

"Thank you," she said, still ruffled from her ungraceful fall in the doorway. She still wondered whether he'd seen it. Maybe it was the gentleman in him that prevented him from mentioning it. She actually looked around, glancing quickly to see where the attractive man who'd helped her up had disappeared to.

A waiter appeared with menus and took their drink orders. She ordered a glass of their house white, he the red, and they chatted about the weather, the tourists, and then about him. He liked to talk about himself —a lot.

"So you're a Red Sox fan, living in Oregon, grew up in Kentucky, one brother, two sisters, you don't like to dance, you raced in a triathlon last year, and you hate the water," she said just as the waiter approached. She took a healthy sip from her glass of wine. It was good, fruity, something different. "Hmm, yummy. How's yours?"

He was watching her. "Ah, haven't tried it." He picked up his glass, took a sip. "Good," he said as the waiter pulled out his notepad to take their orders.

She ordered the restaurant's trademark shrimp dish. Ryder ordered the curry. The waiter left with their menus, and an uncomfortable silence followed, so she took another generous sip of her wine.

He was watching her with light blue eyes, not green. Why did that stranger keep popping into her mind? He wasn't gorgeous like Ryder. No, he had a roughness about him that had been so damn attractive. *Stop thinking about him!*

"I guess I talk a lot about myself. Sorry," he added. "You must think I'm strange, living so close to the ocean but hating it. Never liked boats either—get seasick. What about you?"

"I like the water, boats, being on the ocean. My dad was a commercial fisherman at one time, so you could say I spent a better part of growing up on a boat—"

"Wow, really? I knew a commercial fisherman, was one of my patients. He had bad teeth, crooked, needed bridge work. Very depressed and very negative about life in general, always on about what a crappy year it was, happy only if he could complain about something…"

She couldn't believe he'd cut her off. It was as if he hadn't even heard her, and he was still talking about Joe Shmoe, whom she didn't give two hoots about. Like, seriously?

"Sorry," he said, this time looking about as uncomfortable as she felt. "I can see I'm taking over again. You're so quiet. Tell me about you," he added with enthusiasm.

Really? Talk about putting her on the spot. It was kind of hard to talk when he kept interrupting, and there was something annoying about people who didn't know how to listen. There were, as far as Kate was concerned, two types: those who talked and those who listened. This guy was a talker.

She had to remind herself to try. After all, she had enjoyed their emails back and forth, and the phone chat had been good. He wasn't bad looking even though he was thirty-five. Most important, he had a job, a very good one, a professional career. That said a lot, right? Maybe he was nervous. Yes, that had to be it. First dates always sucked.

"Well," she said, "I know one way to learn about each other is to talk, but as I learned a long time ago, it's not what you say, it's what you do. The first time someone shows you who they are, believe them."

"Wow, very philosophical." He smiled, sitting back and lifting his wine. "I like it. Tell me more about yourself. What do you do?"

"Me? I'm an assistant front desk manager at the Hotel Monaco. I'm single—that's why we're here. I love to jog, play baseball, read. Grew up here in Portland. You know, I find talking about myself really difficult. I do find that getting to know someone is more about spending time with them." She wondered for a moment whether he understood what she was saying. Talkers were quite often just that, all talk. The quiet ones, who were deliberate and just *did*…well, that said a lot about them.

He appeared to consider what she was saying, then smiled again with another uncomfortable silence. Maybe she was boring him, being vague. Hell, she was boring herself trying to think of something exciting and novel to say.

"So," she said, "how come you moved all the way out to Oregon from Kentucky?" *May as well get him talking about himself again.*

"School brought me here. I just stayed after. Married and divorced here," he said.

She tried to remember his profile. It had said single, not divorced. He had never once mentioned anywhere that he had been married. She wondered whether he had kids. Eek, at twenty-two she wasn't looking to be a mom to anyone anytime soon. His profile had said no kids, hadn't it? Now she was struggling to remember what exactly it *had* said.

"Kids?" she asked, and he flashed her that million-dollar smile again.

"Two. I share custody with my ex. They're five and ten, cute as buttons. Here." He reached into his pocket and pulled out his wallet, flipping to the photos. He was right, they were cute—and so was the woman standing behind them. Not cute, gorgeous. She had long red hair, a great figure.

"Your ex in the photo?" Her voice sounded off, but that had to be the shock of realizing she'd been hoodwinked again, or so it seemed as she stared at the family photo that had them appearing so happy.

"Yeah, that's Jenna. Great mother to my kids, and I'll always love her, but we were just never right for each other—like oil and water."

Unbelievable. How dense could this guy be, showing his date a photo of another woman with his kids—whom he'd neglected to mention? That was just so wrong.

"So why'd you two break up, if you don't mind me asking?" She had a feeling, watching how cavalier he was, that he was considering what to say.

He shrugged sharply as he lifted his glass of wine, swirling the liquid. "Stuff happens, you know. I was busy with my career, and she wanted something different, something more than I could give her." He was quiet again and looked down into his wine. Now who was being coy?

"What, did you cheat?" she said. She was kidding, really, but he was being awfully closemouthed after offering so much information about himself moments before. It took her a second to realize she'd hit the nail on the head, because he wasn't laughing.

"We all do things we're not proud of. It was a momentary lapse. It meant nothing."

Oh my good God, she thought. He wasn't kidding. So he was one of those fuckers. Her dad had been a cheater, always sorry, and then he'd even cheat on the one he'd been cheating with. Kate had watched the merry-go-round of her parents' marriage: her mom leaving, then going back. She'd spent most of her teenage years feeling as if she were a yo-yo, bouncing back and forth.

"It was one time, Kate. I'm not one of those guys." When he looked at her, it was the first time she felt as if he really meant what he was saying. He'd suddenly become serious. "I screwed up. My wife and I had been fighting. She'd given everything to the baby, completely ignoring me. I was being a selfish bastard because my needs weren't being met, and we drifted apart. I was lonely, so I did something I wasn't proud of. I signed up on an online dating site, looking for…I don't know what I was looking for, really, but I asked for something casual, and that was where I met her. It was supposed to be no names, just a hookup. I never expected to hear from her again, and that would be the end of it. Felt like crap too, after."

She didn't know what to say, so she swallowed more wine and waited, as he seemed to be thinking some pretty heavy thoughts. Gone was his killer smile. He chugged the rest of his wine and slid the glass to the edge of the table, flagging the waiter and gesturing to his glass for another. Of course she didn't miss how tense he'd become.

"I heard that many guys who sign up online are married even though they say they're not," she said.

He gave her a look as he leaned back. "It's true, many are. Men can be dirty dogs, you know. It's not an excuse. What I did was deplorable, and I paid the price, but I'm not the same guy."

"Oh?" What could she say as she started ticking off all the strikes against him? He had lied about his age in a big way, lied about not having been married and the fact that he had kids… What else in his profile was false, she wondered?

"She showed up at my office," he said, dragging her

from her thoughts as she tried to think about whether she could skip dessert with the excuse that she had to work early.

"Who?" It took her a minute to realize he was talking about either his wife or the other woman.

He flicked his gaze to her, and gone was the lightness she'd seen there moments ago. No, she could see the weight of something he was carrying as he took his hand and wiped it across his chin. "The woman from online. Two days later, she showed up, sitting in a chair at my dental office when I walked in, getting readied by one of my hygienists. I thought, what are the odds she was suddenly a new patient? That was a line I never crossed, bringing my personal bullshit into the office. But I let it go and kept it light, worried that my hygienist would pick up on what I'd done.

"I gave her the quickest checkup I could and got her the hell out of there, and I made sure my receptionist understood that she was to be referred to another dentist if she called back, with strict instructions that we wouldn't be able to accommodate her. Of course they had to be wondering what the hell was going on, but at least they didn't ask. Then she somehow got my cell number, the one I don't give out to anyone but friends and my staff at work. One night she was waiting by my car as I closed up for the night."

"Holy shit, that sounds very stalkerish," Kate said. She couldn't believe a woman would stoop to that, and for a second she felt sorry for Ryder.

He rubbed his hand over the back of his neck. "Yeah, well, it was starting to really piss me off, and I told her to back off or I was going to call the cops."

"Did you?"

He shook his head. "Not right away. I should have, but I was too worried about having something official out there for my wife to find out."

So he really had cheated on his wife and then stayed with her as if he'd done nothing wrong. Bastard! "That's so awful. I can't believe you had to threaten her with the cops. I've heard of this happening, but…"

"She didn't go away," he said.

She wondered if her jaw could drop any lower.

"Then one day I came home, and she was holding my six-month-old baby daughter. She was in my house. My wife walked into the living room with tea as if they were the best of friends, introducing her to me. I was watching this crazy woman—Cindy was her name—and I realized then, I'm so totally screwed. This woman wasn't going away. I pulled her aside when my wife was down the hall changing the baby, and I asked her what the hell she was doing in my house, with my wife. She touched me and said if I hadn't ignored her calls, she wouldn't have approached my wife at all. She had the gall to say they met in the park. And you know what really scared me?"

Ryder glanced up at the waiter, who set another glass of red in front of him. He smiled politely, took another swallow of wine, and then flicked his gaze, all serious now, back to Kate. "She talked about my oldest daughter, and she knew things about her: where she went to school, what she'd worn the other day, things I hadn't even realized about my own kid. It was enough that I knew she'd been watching my kid, my family, my house. I knew then that I couldn't ignore her, or this, anymore. So I called the cops, told my wife, and my marriage was over. That same night, I was packing my bags and moving out. The cops went and talked with her one on one and told her to go away and stop bugging me. Then I got a restraining order. She was good for a while. She stayed away."

Gone was the happy, charming Ryder. This Ryder was humbled, not the cocky bullshitter who had been sitting there moments before. Kate really did feel kind of sorry for the guy. Although she didn't like cheaters, what Cindy had done was almost psychotic and way over the top. *Talk about learning your lesson!* "You mean she kept coming around, broke the restraining order?"

"Not in a way that the police could arrest her, but yeah. Just far enough away."

"Well, what did this woman want?"

"Me," he said, and it wasn't arrogant or cocky. It was sad and pathetic.

She didn't know what made her look—the flash of lights she caught from the corner of her eye or the sedan squealing and speeding up onto the sidewalk through the front window, coming right toward them. In that moment, when time froze, she saw every detail: the car, the GM logo on the front, the person behind the wheel, the shattered glass, the dishes on the table, the screams, the shouts…

However it happened, the next thing she knew, she was on the ground. In a moment of quiet, she looked up at the carnage from the floor.

CHAPTER
Three

He was considering having a second Guinness. He wasn't in the mood for talking tonight, and he said a quick goodnight to Febriski, the desk sergeant, as he leaned against the light cedar block of the bar.

"Another, Walker?"

He liked Jean, the short blonde who was part owner of this trendy club. The food was good, the drinks were cold, and it was close to the precinct. "Yeah, sure, why not?"

She pulled the bottle from the fridge, cracked the cap, and set it on the counter. She went to slide him a clean glass, but he waved her off.

"Business looks good," he said, taking in the crowd, all suits. This location attracted a certain clientele.

She gave him a sly smile. "Business has been phenomenal. Packed every night. Reservations are currently a three-week waitlist, and we had the local paper here doing a write up in the food section. All that great publicity helps." She tapped the counter and gestured to one of the wait staff, who took over behind the bar.

"Your brother's the chef, right?" Walker said. He still couldn't believe the brother-sister team had paired up and opened this successful restaurant. 525 was the talk of the town.

"Vince is the genius behind all those dishes on the menu. He always could cook back when we were kids. Took over from Mom, who couldn't cook if her life depended on it. I think then it was more about survival."

He swallowed the dark brew. "How old is he again?"

"Twenty-three."

"You're twins, right?" he asked. Jean was a pistol, a self-starter, and he wanted to get to know her better. If she was anything in bed like she was running this establishment, hell, she'd be a firecracker.

"You know we are, old man."

"Ouch." He touched his heart with the flat of his palm. "I have, what, five years on you?"

"Are you hitting on me again?" she said. For such a young thing, she was far from shy. That could turn an otherwise boring night into a good time he was sure he'd remember fondly. He wondered whether she was one of those take-charge types, a wildfire who'd have him begging, sweating, and doing his damnedest to keep up. God, he hoped so.

"And if I am, are you going to turn me down again, or are you going to finally give in to what we both know you really want?"

She jabbed her finger into his arm. His dress shirt was rolled up to his sleeves, his .45 clipped to his belt. "What if I told you I was seeing someone?" she said.

"Are you?" he said. Had she really been seeing

someone else all these times he'd been hitting on her, almost every night for the past month? "Can't be that serious, as I know you're considering letting me have my way with you, and I'm breaking you down. I can see it every day. I'm making headway, and one night you're going to walk out of here with me, because you and I both know it'll be a night you'll never forget."

Her mischievous smile was bright and so catlike. He'd give anything to know what was going on in her mind. Then she tilted her head, really studying him. "So what exactly are you looking for, Walker? Because I'm not too interested in dating a cop."

"Who said anything about dating?" He rested his arms on the bar, and she licked her lower lip. The sizzle between them in that moment had him hardening. He wanted to taste her, to bite her lip, to put his mouth on the soft pink spot that still glistened from where she'd licked it. Then he pictured her mouth on him, those lips around him.

"No." She slapped the counter and pushed away. "But thanks for the offer."

"Tease," he said as he reached for his beer and drank down the last of it, for a moment feeling absolutely miserable.

She laughed, wagging her finger at him before walking away. "Same time tomorrow night," she called.

He set his empty on the counter and tossed down some bills. "Not tomorrow, I have the night shift. Take care, Jean. Let me know if anyone hassles you."

She jutted her chin toward him, and her expression softened. "Stay safe out there, Walker."

Good God, he really did want to get to know her better. She interested the hell out of him. He liked her and the flirtatious banter they'd had going on now for months. She was smart, sexy, had a great sense of humor, and she could hold her own with her crowd of diners. Whoever the lucky dog was who'd finally snag her, well, Walker was envious.

He shrugged on his navy sports coat and stopped in the crowded waiting area, glancing into the dining room. He didn't know why he noticed her, the babe in those killer heels and red dress sitting with the dude with the slick hair and phony smile. What was it with women, always going for the flash, charm, and good looks? Then he heard something that had him stepping further inside. Through the window, he could see a car speeding up onto the sidewalk between two parked cars, heading right for the chick in the red dress. Everything went into slow motion, and she looked up just as the car crashed through the front glass of Portland's hottest restaurant.

Four

"What the fuck?" he cried. Even before it registered in his overtired brain, he was moving. The fact was that some idiot had just crashed up his friend's restaurant—and who knew how many people had been injured? The good-looking broad in the red dress, he feared, was most likely dead. He stepped over broken glass and slipped on something gooey on the floor. In an instant, he assessed the dust and debris. A man on the floor was crawling, a cut on his head, helping up a woman who had lettuce in her hair.

"Are you hurt?" Walker demanded as he touched the man, who looked shocked. Hell, everyone had to be. They had all been out for a nice dinner and then *wham* —some idiot had driven a car through the front of the restaurant. He guessed no one would be paying their tabs that night.

"I'm okay, just—what the fuck happened…?" the woman screeched, reaching for her purse.

One of the waiters appeared, and then someone else, to help the woman. More waiters and staff raced out from the back, helping people up. Those who could stand began heading around the debris to the door.

"Oh my God, my restaurant!" Jean cried out behind him. He could only imagine her horror.

"Get everyone outside," he shouted. He could hear the sirens in the distance, coming closer. He stepped around the car, hoping to hell no one was under it. He helped patrons as they staggered from the once fine restaurant, which now resembled a war zone. But he still didn't see the blonde.

A tabletop shuddered in the corner, and Walker lifted it off a man: oh, yeah, the slick, smiling dude who'd been sitting with the girl in the red dress. "Are you hurt?" Walker asked.

The man was covered in dust and debris as he brushed off his coat and coughed, then struggled to stand. "Holy crap, what the hell?" He was looking around.

Walker heard a cough, then saw the blonde crawling again on her knees from the corner and around an overturned table.

"Kate, are you okay?" the slick dude asked—but Walker got to her first.

She was a mess. Her knee was cut, her dress torn at the shoulder, and she was wearing one shoe.

"Are you all right?" He touched her arm and helped her up, taking in the shock on her face the moment she saw him. Why hadn't he noticed before how lovely her eyes were, a smoky brown, big and bold? She held on to his arm as if needing support. He could feel how shaky she was.

"What happened? I saw the car…" She stopped and pointed. The way her eyes widened had Walker turning as he heard the squeal of the car door. There was shouting, and others crowded around, helping a woman out of the vehicle. She was dark haired, a little dazed. Walker could feel the woman Slick had called Kate as she dug her fingers into his arm.

"Oh, my dress," she cried. She grabbed the drooping strap that had slipped to show black lace and the rounded curve of her breast. And a nice breast it was, too—especially in the fancy bra responsible for all that generous cleavage.

He was about to slip off his jacket and offer it when he realized she was with Slick. He should have been shedding his coat and handing it over, but instead he was looking the other way. Walker glanced over to the dude, who was staring open mouthed at the woman getting out of the car.

"Cindy?" he said.

"Ryder, do you know her?" Kate asked, holding up the strap of her dress.

"That would be Cindy, remember? I was just telling you about her."

"The woman you met online, who was stalking you?" Kate staggered a bit, balancing on one heel. Walker noticed a stain on her dress.

"Excuse me, you know this woman?" he asked. He was starting to wonder what the hell was going on.

"Ryder, is that you?" the woman called out, her hand on the door of the wrecked sedan. She didn't have a mark on her. She tucked her long dark hair behind her ears and then smiled over at Slick as if this was just an everyday occurrence and they'd simply run into each other. Good God, this was going to be a nightmare.

"Cindy, are you following me?" Slick sounded really

pissed. Hell, Walker was pissed, because although people talked about coincidences, he didn't believe in them. Not at all.

"What? No, what happened?" She put her hand to her head and weaved a bit. Either she was a really good actor or she was hurt. "Oh my God, this is awful," she cried.

"You have got to be kidding me. Seriously?" Slick said.

Walker didn't know where to look: at the outrage on Kate's face or at this Ryder dude she was with, who appeared a little frightened and really annoyed.

"You know her?" Walker asked Kate, who was now shaking her head and still holding up her dress strap.

"I don't, but it seems my date does. Man, I cannot win with men. What are the odds the woman he picked up on the net for a one nighter is now stalking him and drove a car right through the front of a restaurant where I was sitting with him? I'll tell you what it is. It's karma or some bullshit fucked-up nightmare that's telling me I can't pick a guy if my life depended on it."

Walker slipped off his jacket and held it out to Kate as he asked Ryder, "Is that true? She stalking you?"

Kate accepted his jacket and slipped it on. He kind of felt sorry for her.

"Yes, ended my marriage, she did," Ryder said. "Won't leave me alone. She just keeps showing up. Holy God, did she try to kill me?" He didn't move but also made no effort to console his date—a date with killer legs, a tight ass, and the perfect curves poured into an amazing red dress, the kind of dress Walker would have loved to peel off after a night on the town, anticipating what was to come. Something so sweet, sweaty, and satisfying.

"What's your name?" he asked.

"Ryder Connelly." He went to hold out his hand, and Walker looked down at it as he put both hands on his hips, thumbing the gun clipped to his belt. Ryder obviously thought better of reaching out and touching a cop, as he squeezed his fist and lowered his hand. "Oh, and this is Kate—I'm sorry, what was your last name?"

Smooth dude. Walker noticed the way Kate bristled. What was it exactly that she saw in this joker, anyway? She was obviously now seeing him as Walker did. Maybe she was smarter than he'd given her credit for, after all.

"Kate Sikes," she said a little sharply. "We met online. Evidently, I still can't pick 'em."

Ryder gave her a sour look. "Hey, look, it wasn't as if I was going to ask you out a second time."

"Yeah, you were just looking for another one nighter. Guess you haven't learned." She glanced over to Cindy, who was now pushing away from the waiters and people around her. Two uniformed cops walked in and gestured to Walker. He pointed at Cindy, and they stopped her from taking another step.

"You get a restraining order against her?" he asked Ryder, but he didn't miss the way Kate rolled her eyes. He was sure she had to be thinking what an idiot this guy was. He hoped she realized guys like this slick were often more talk than action, but then he felt sorry for the dude with a broad stalking him. That was downright creepy.

Ryder was looking truly miserable. "For all the good it's done. She won't leave me alone. Not a week goes by that she doesn't turn up where I am—the coffee shop, the newspaper stand, even my gym. She was suddenly there. I quit the gym and lost the money I paid for the membership. She always just stays that thousand feet from me. No more, no less. I want it to stop!" he shouted. "Get the hell out of my life!"

Walker stepped away from Kate to the uniformed officers, who were talking to the stalker broad. "Take her in for questioning," he said. "I'm not liking this. I'll be right in. Have the paramedics check her out, though, too."

He walked back over to Kate, who was still wearing his jacket, a mess, and was now lifting a chair and part of a table. "What are you doing?" he asked.

"Looking for my shoe so I can go home and try to forget this disaster of a night."

"Well, that's the thing. You can't go home. I need a statement from you. I need both of you to come to the station."

"For what?" She stood up, lifting one of those sexy black fuck-me heels and leaning against the wall to take off the other. She now stood barefoot, glaring over at Ryder and then him.

"Well, for one, the car she drove through the front window was coming right for you."

Maybe she hadn't realized what Walker had already figured out. Her face paled, and those sharp amber eyes that a moment ago had been filled with outrage now shone with fear.

CHAPTER
Five

"I can't believe this is happening," Jean said.

Walker handed a napkin to her as she sat on a stool in the now empty bar. Emergency lights flashed outside, and crowds of people milled around, watching the accident scene much like they would have watched a train wreck. Her brother, the chef, was on the phone with someone. He was upset, rightly so, and slammed the receiver down. Crime scene had arrived and had taped off the area, and witnesses were now having their statements taken.

It was clear that the woman had driven straight into the restaurant, but no one could say whether she had simply lost control or it was deliberate. Tire tracks showed she hadn't swerved, but he couldn't say either way for sure.

"I'm sorry, Jean," he said. "This is shitty."

She dried her eyes, about ready to start crying again, but Walker wasn't the type to console a woman in despair. This was when he got itchy feet and found an excuse to slip away. Some guys were good at this, but

Walker liked women who could hold it together. Emotions made things messy.

"Shitty? It's criminal," she said. "Now what's going to happen? We'll be closed for how long, and what the hell are you doing with the woman who ran into my place? Who's going to pay for this?"

"You need to call your insurance company," he said. "I feel for you, Jean, but there's nothing more you can do tonight. You should go home. We'll let you know when we're through here."

"Are you kidding? So now the cops are going to hold my restaurant hostage and decide when I can start getting in here and fixing things up? I want that car pulled out of here now so we can get repairs started and have this restaurant open again in a few days." She sounded determined and bossy. "Every day we're closed, I lose money, reservations are cancelled, and wages are lost, not to mention food is wasted…" She was going on and on, and he wondered at what point he had tuned her out, as she kept slapping her hand to emphasize each statement.

He didn't have the heart to tell her things just weren't going to go her way. "Jean, go home," he said. "Do you need a ride?"

"No, Walker, I have my car in back."

"Detective!" one of the officers on scene called out, walking toward him. "Kate is wanting to go home, and Ryder Connelly has asked for a timeframe of when they can give their statements."

Walker turned to the uniformed officer who had been first on the scene. He had dark hair and was young, of average height. He couldn't remember his name, so he glanced down at the tag on his uniform.

MacDonald. "Take them to the station, MacDonald. I'll be right behind you. Do you have statements from all the witnesses?"

The young cop flipped through his notebook. "Just an elderly couple left, but we have names and contact information for everyone who was here. Oh, and paramedics checked over the driver and cleared her. Other than being a little shaken up, there wasn't a bump on her. She was taken down to the station already."

"Great, thank you. Jean, you going to be okay?" Walker asked. He hated leaving her like this. He felt bad even though none of this was his fault.

She waved a tearstained napkin at him. "Go, I'll be fine."

"Jean, are you okay?" someone shouted. "Oh my God, I just heard!"

Walker turned as a light-haired young man with glasses, a leather coat, and blue jeans hurried in. He held out his arms, and Walker watched as Jean stood up, her face crumbling into another fit of tears as she walked into the man's arms. He was much younger than Walker. He looked as if he was just out of high school, but he was probably closer to Jean's age. By the way the man held her, Walker realized that all his own flirtatious banter would never have gone anywhere.

He didn't hear what Jean said as he started out of the bar with MacDonald and spotted Kate in the foyer, sitting barefoot, wearing his coat, and Slick about as far away from her as he could get. Walker gestured to Ryder with his chin and told MacDonald, "Take him, and I'll take Kate down."

She was now glaring up at him, and he noticed she had a scrape on the side of her chin.

"You have no idea how lucky you are that you weren't injured," he said. "From where you were sitting, I half expected things to turn out a lot worse than they did. You are one fortunate young woman."

"You think I'm fortunate? I've got to tell you, from where I see it, I think this is the universe's way of flipping me the bird. So no, thank you, I'm not lucky. I am so far from lucky. All the expense—the shoes, the dress, my hair…so I think I won't agree with you."

He wondered whether she was thinking of something else to add when she stopped and took a breath. "Look on the bright side," he said. "At least this saved you the wasted time of having a relationship that was headed down a one-way street to nowhere."

She rolled her eyes. "Spoken like someone who has no clue what it's like to date in the real world. Can we go, please? Just take my statement. Why can't you do it here? It's not as if you're hauling everyone in this restaurant down to the station. No, I think I might just decline. I'd really like to go home."

He held out his hand. "Well, that's not an option. You're coming. Just think of yourself as special. Come on, I'll drive you. Car's not parked far." He glanced down at her bare feet. "You might want to put your shoes back on. Can you walk in them?"

"Yes, I can walk in them." She slipped her shoes back on, and he noticed, as she rose on those stilts and wobbled a bit, that she might not be as steady as she'd let on. He often wondered how women could walk in shoes that high without breaking their necks or at least their ankles.

Maybe that was why he held out his arm for her to take.

"I can walk, just so you know," she said. Nonetheless, she slipped her hand over his arm and held on. "I'm just shaky from all that happened. I'm not a total klutz."

In those heels, she was almost his height. There was something about long legs and a woman whose eyes he could look right into without having to look down at her that really appealed to him. He held the door, and she walked beside him, holding on tight, so close that her leg and hip were brushing against him. Then she leaned closer and—Jesus, it really had been a long time since he'd been with a woman, because he was having all kinds of indecent thoughts about leaning her against his car and running his hand up the side of her thigh, over the curve of her generously rounded ass… *Stop it!* He was going to be a fine mess if he allowed himself to keep thinking of Kate in such an inappropriate, X-rated way. For all he knew, she could be some psycho nutcase too.

He opened the back door, and she froze beside him, letting go of his arm and crossing hers over her generous bust. She glanced up at him with a look he easily deciphered. The woman was digging her heels in and had no intention of getting into the car.

"What am I, a criminal?" She gestured to the backseat.

He slammed the backdoor. "Sorry, habit," he said before opening the passenger door. This time, she climbed in and reached for the handle to pull it closed herself.

The woman didn't just ignore him, she held her chin up as she stared out the front windshield as if he didn't even exist. *Bitch,* he thought as he strode around to his side and climbed in.

"Fasten your seatbelt, or are you going to argue with me about how you have no intention of wearing it?"

She didn't look at him as she clicked her belt in place.

He started the car, punched it in gear, and gunned it a little harder than was strictly necessary.

CHAPTER

Six

"She says she'll only talk to you," MacDonald said. He stood about four inches shorter than Walker's five foot eleven, but he was young and pumped, always wearing short sleeves—maybe to show off those bulging biceps he had to be proud of.

Walker had just left the interview room where Cindy Schmidt was being held. He glanced back through the one-way glass to where another detective, Kruso—a short redhead, married, with a brood of kids—continued to talk to the distraught woman.

"Great, where is she?" he asked sarcastically.

"I moved her to interview one. She demanded a tea, herbal with no caffeine, and she's hungry. Asked if we had a salad or something light she could eat since the car that drove through the restaurant arrived before she'd actually had dinner."

He laughed. "Seriously, who does she think we are?"

MacDonald shrugged. "Just telling you what she said. I told her no, tried to get the statement, and that was when she demanded to see you. What do you want me to do?"

Kate was beginning to sound like a pain in the ass. Walker let out a sigh he knew sounded annoyed. Hell, he *was* annoyed. Couldn't she just give her damn statement and then get out of his hair? "I'll talk to her," he said.

"What about her demands for food and tea?"

Walker turned to the cop and stared at him. "You planning on whipping up a salad?" He gestured toward the station's break room.

"No, was going to grab someone's leftover sandwich from the fridge."

Walker was speechless. "And do we really have that herbal crap here?"

MacDonald just looked at him. "I don't know, was just going to grab whatever I saw and give it to her."

Walker just shook his head. "No, don't. I'll deal with her."

He opened the door to the interview room. Kate was sitting in the hard-back chair in which criminals usually sat. He wondered why she had been brought in here. Maybe he needed to have a word with MacDonald. After all, he'd left Kate sitting at his desk—but then, he was pretty sure being a pain in the ass was what had landed her in here.

"Well, it's about time." She crossed her arms. "Is this how you treat everyone you need a statement from, or just those who've almost been run down? I'm the victim here, am I not?"

Walker shut the door and took in the pad of paper and pen sitting in front of Kate. He strode over to the chair across from her and pulled it out. Her eyes were deep brown and seemed to dance with gold around them. He'd never seen eyes the color of hers before, and that hair…even after crawling out of that debris, she had gold highlights he loved. The color seemed to match her eyes.

"We were full up, trying to give you some privacy," he said, though he knew that was bullshit. Evidently, Kate had pushed the wrong buttons with MacDonald, so he'd moved her to less comfortable surroundings.

She slid the yellow lined pad of paper toward him. He took in the full page of neat penmanship with that day's date filled in at the top. "Here's your statement," she said. "Do you want to go over anything else with me, or can I go now?" She leaned forward, tightly wound.

When was the last time she got laid? he couldn't help wondering. "Well, just let me have a look here and make sure you've left nothing out."

He should have been hurrying to get her out of there, out of his hair. What the hell was the matter with him, keeping her there? At times, he wondered why he seemed to get himself embroiled in such grief. This woman, he had no doubt, could be the end of a man.

She took a slightly exaggerated breath, and he glanced her way. She widened her eyes at him. "What?" she snapped.

He just shook his head as he glanced back to her very detailed description of her conversation with Ryder Connelly while sitting at the table. How this was their first date, how they'd met online, how many emails they'd exchanged, how she'd met Ryder for the first time at the restaurant, and a word-for-word transcription of their conversation, including the moment when she saw the car right before it crashed through the restaurant window. He flipped over the paper, realizing she had written four pages. "You're very detailed," he said as he read.

"It's my job. I have to be. It helps to pay attention, which is what I do. I notice things about people so as to avoid potential problems."

"So what job has you paying this much attention?"

"I'm the assistant front desk manager at the Hotel Monaco. Now can I go home?" She was direct.

"I can have one of the uniformed officers drive you." He pushed back his chair, and for the first time she appeared very much alone as she glanced down and seemed to soften from the tough-girl attitude she'd been carrying since walking into the station.

"I'm sorry if I've been a little sharp with everyone," she said. "Did she really drive into the restaurant heading right for me?" There was a slight hitch in her voice.

Walker rested his hand on the back of the chair. "From what I saw."

"That was just a coincidence, right? I mean, are you sure it wasn't Ryder she was trying to take out? I just happened to be sitting at the same table with him, and it was a big car."

Why hadn't he seen it before? This woman wasn't so black and white. At times, when people were scared, they said and did things that made them seem prickly—which he had no doubt she was to begin with, but there was something else about Kate Sikes that bothered Walker in a way no other woman had. For a minute, he found himself wanting to protect her.

She glanced away and then stiffened. "You know what? I would really like to go home now." Her tone had suddenly become frosty again, as if she had recovered from momentarily forgetting she was supposed to be a bitch. What the hell was it with women? First warm, then cold.

"Fine, I'll have an officer have you out of here shortly. Oh, and in case you're wondering, your boyfriend gave his statement and was out of here an hour ago."

She didn't say a word as she looked over at him, the hardness fully back in her expression. "Let's get this straight: he's not my boyfriend. Do I really want to know why you kept me here and had him out before me when he's responsible for this?" She gestured to the door. Oh, was she pissed.

"Well, I'm pretty sure it had more to do with the fact that he was more cooperative than you, and he wasn't a pain in the ass," Walker said, and he heard her gasp as he pulled open the door. He listened to it click closed behind him, leaving Kate locked in the interrogation room.

K ate unlocked the door to her fifth-floor apartment. She was barefoot, carrying the over-priced shoes she was tempted to toss in the trash. At the time, she had considered them to be an investment, well worth the expense of $169, as they made her long, slender legs appear shapely and her ass a piece of art, as the shop girl had commented. She had agreed and spent the money, deciding that eating salad for a week was a worthwhile tradeoff.

Maybe she'd reconsider—tossing the shoes, that is. But then, she had a lot to reconsider after the date she'd set so many of her hopes on, which had turned into a disaster of epic proportions. She reminded herself, after hours at the police station and then stuck in a smelly interrogation room, filling out a report, that she was hopeless at picking men. Afterward, she'd demanded to see Detective Walker Pruett, who barely looked at her statement before leaving her locked in the same stinking interrogation room, with concrete walls, one-way glass, and bars on the window.

She tried to tell herself she wasn't attracted to such a pompous ass, but the truth was that the only reason she'd demanded to see the arrogant redheaded, green-eyed handsome devil was that he had left an impression on her, and she couldn't help wanting to get to know him better. Even though he spurred her blood and had her acting like a world-class bitch—which she wasn't—he was the only one in that entire mess who had come to her rescue. Yes, that arrogant, cocky detective had picked her up from the floor not once but twice, and how had she acted toward him? Like a spoiled child.

She pulled at the edge of Detective Pruett's sports coat, which she was still wearing even after having been driven home by a uniformed officer who'd dropped her off at the front door and pulled away before she even opened it. Served her right. It was sobering to reflect on her behavior. She hadn't set eyes on Detective Pruett again after he left her cooling her heels in the interview room—literally, since she had taken her shoes off after arriving at the station.

She could have left the coat, but in the chaos of the restaurant disaster, she hadn't thought to look for hers, and with her ruined strap, she felt half naked. She hadn't been interested in parading through an over-crowded police station, having to hold up a strap to keep herself together. She'd been irritated—no, mad that the cop had made her come in and then wait at a desk as if she were some criminal. She had been furi-ous, but at the same time she hadn't been able to help noticing how the man's green eyes against the red of his hair made him unusually striking. She'd always gone for the pretty-boy type, which Detective Pruett was so far from, but something rough and rugged about him had her wanting him more than she had any man.

"Stop it!" she snapped at herself. Maybe Pruett was the type who expected to have his way in everything. It was in the way he talked, the way he walked. He seemed the type, a man who knew how to look after himself, not too tall but tall enough, the kind of guy whose eyes she could get lost in, the kind whose arms she knew could hold her. Of course she had noticed his hands: broad, large, capable, a working man's hands—and no ring.

"Jerk." She dropped her shoes at the door and her purse on the counter and slipped off his coat, resting it over the back of her gold sectional before stripping out of her ruined dress, leaving it in a pool in the hallway. She unfastened her black strapless bra, dropped it where she was, and stepped out of her matching lace underwear, leaving a trail of clothes as she flicked on the light to her bedroom and froze. There, written in red across the wall over her bed, in block letters, were the words YOU CAN'T HAVE HIM BITCH.

She covered her breasts with her hands and screamed, then searched for something to put on. She spied the blanket at the foot of the bed and wrapped it around herself as she raced into the kitchen and fumbled in her purse for her cellphone. Detective Pruett's card slipped out. She'd grabbed it from his desk before being moved to one of the rooms reserved for hardened criminals. She was no longer mad—she was freaking out, looking around her apartment, taking everything in: the bookshelf, the closed curtains, the small living room with magazines and books stacked on the coffee table.

Think, think, has anything been moved? She couldn't

remember how'd she'd left it, but the feeling of having been invaded made her back up against the fridge, listening to every creak as his phone rang. "Please pick up. Come on, Detective. Please be there."

She was still praying he would answer when his deep voice barked, "Pruett."

"Hello? This is Kate Sikes, from the police station. I got your card—I mean, I was at the restaurant…" Damn, she was rambling.

"Kate," he said, his voice warming. "You left with something of mine."

"Someone was in my apartment," she said. "I think it was that crazy woman who drove into the restaurant." Her voice was shaking.

"What do you mean, someone was in your place? Are they still there?"

"No, I don't know. I just got home and walked into my bedroom, and written across my wall above my bed is 'You can't have him, bitch.'" She couldn't believe it. She was looking over her shoulder with that creeped-out feeling she got whenever she felt as if someone was watching her.

"Give me your address," he snapped.

She heard him say something to someone in the background as she rattled off the address. She gripped the blanket around herself tighter, holding it up.

"Kate, are you there?" He was back on the line.

"Yeah, just hanging here," she said.

"Get out of your apartment now," he said. "I've got a unit on the way, and so am I."

She didn't need him to tell her twice. She crept down the hallway, her heart hammering as she pulled open the door and raced out, holding the phone and the blanket. She started for the stairs, but her apartment door slammed shut just as someone ripped her blanket away. She screamed and turned. "Oh shit, oh no!" she cried.

"What's going on?" Detective Pruett yelled on the other end.

"Oh no!" She held the phone away, staring at the blanket—it was just caught in the door—and she could hear the detective yelling, calling her name over and over as she grabbed the knob and turned. Damn door was locked!

She heard the door across the hall unlock, and she dropped the phone, using one hand to cover her breasts and the other to cover her private parts as the door opened and Mr. Harris, her retired schoolteacher neighbor, stood in the entrance of his apartment.

His eyes widened, and he said, "Oh my."

She stared at the phone, her phone, on the floor. She could hear Pruett yelling, "Kate, what the hell's going on? Kate!" She looked up to Mr. Harris, who was now holding a towel. Before he turned his head, he tossed it her way.

Eight

W alker arrived at the apartment right behind a cruiser carrying the two uniformed officers he'd dispatched. They were first to the door, and an elderly black man with white hair opened it. He was in his pajamas, wearing a plaid red housecoat overtop.

"She's upstairs in my apartment, fifth floor. Door's open," the man said.

The two officers started up the stairs.

"Just so you know, I didn't touch her."

That had Pruett turning to look at the man, who appeared worried.

"Don't know what's going on, but when I opened my apartment door after hearing a scream, she was standing there as naked as the day she was born. I tossed her a towel and let her wait in my place. She told me the police were coming. Just wanted you to know I didn't touch her. I came down here and waited for you."

Naked, what the hell? Walker shook his head, sympathizing with the man. It must have been a shock to open his door to find a naked white woman young enough to be his daughter or granddaughter. Walker pointed up the stairs. "Up there?"

"That's right, fifth floor. Apartment door's open," he said again as if Walker needed to be reminded. "If you don't mind, I'll wait on down here." Boy, did the man look uncomfortable.

"Did you see anyone go in her place?"

The man shook his head. "No. She was rambling on about someone being inside and writing on the wall above her bed. She was pretty freaked out. I haven't seen anyone, but I don't pay much attention to who's coming or going. The walls are thin. Heard her go out, but didn't hear anything or anyone else."

"I'll send one of the officers down to take your statement," Walker said. He really did feel bad, considering he'd already experienced Kate at her finest earlier this evening. "Don't worry, I told her to get out of her place," he told the man. "But why naked?" he added, more to himself, as he started up the stairs and looked back down at the elderly neighbor. Considering the time of night, Walker thought he was handling the situation really well.

He stopped at the open door and followed the officers inside. They were staring down at Kate, who had wrapped a light brown towel around herself. It didn't hide much, but, sitting down, at least she was somewhat covered.

"Dare I ask what happened?" Walker said, gesturing to her state of undress.

She flushed. "I had a blanket around me when I called you, and somehow it got stuck in the door. When the door shut, I locked myself out. I can't believe this is happening to me. First the worst date of my life—and I thought there was a possibility with that guy—and then some psycho chick drives through the restaurant, damn near kills me, and someone was in my place, wrote above my bed…"

"Anyone there?" He knew she was going to go on and on if he didn't shut her up.

"I didn't stick around to find out. That's kind of why I'm in this position." Now she just sounded nasty.

"You always walk around naked?" he said. Oh, why had he asked? Just picturing her walking around her apartment without a stitch of anything on was doing all kinds of things to him and making him uncomfortable. One of the officers smirked but didn't say anything.

She gave him a scathing look, but all she said was "Are you going to go find out who did it and if they're still here?"

He couldn't help smiling at the firecracker sitting on the old leather sofa, but he was also pretty sure whoever had been in her apartment was long gone. "You got a key?" he said. He didn't know what had made him ask, but the look she gave him made it all worth it. What was it about her that made him want to go a round or two? She was the kind of woman that burned with passion and fire. There were some he looked forward to sparring with, to getting a rise out of. He imagined the makeup sex would be worth the frustration he was sure that woman could put a man through.

"You really think I would be sitting here in this predicament if I had my key?" She was about to stand up, he could tell, but then thought better of it.

He chuckled under his breath and left one of the uniformed cops with her. The first thing he noticed when he stepped out of the apartment was her cell phone on the floor and a cream-colored blanket caught in the door. Walker took less than a minute to open it. He pulled his Glock from his holster and pushed the door open. The lights were on as he stepped in, one of the officers behind him. The first thing he noticed was the red dress, black bra, and underwear on the floor. Otherwise, her apartment was reasonably neat.

"You check the living room," he said to the cop behind him. He opened one closet door and then the bathroom, flicking on the light, but he saw nothing. When he went into the bedroom, he saw the writing on the wall above the bed. Creepy, it was. He checked the bedroom closet, jam packed with clothes, before walking over to the bold lettering. Upon looking close, he was positive whoever wrote it had used the tube of red lipstick that was sitting on the edge of the nightstand. YOU CAN'T HAVE HIM BITCH.

"All clear out here," one of the officers said, the one who'd driven Kate home earlier. "Whoever was here isn't now. Holy shit, look at that. Someone doesn't like her. Do you think it's her pleasing personality?"

"You know what? That girl across the hall may be a pain in the ass, but she's scared, and I'm pretty sure that's her way of putting on a tough face." Walker was convinced most of Kate's snarky attitude was her way of protecting herself. Maybe she had been put in that position one too many times.

"Sorry," the officer said.

Walker glanced his way and then moved past him and out of the room. "Seal it off. Let's get crime scene techs down here to dust for prints and find out who did this." He started out into the hallway before spying his jacket draped over the back of the sofa. He reached for it and then left the apartment, picking up the blanket on the floor.

The elderly man was just now coming up the stairs. "Everything okay?" he said. "Was someone bothering that girl?" He sounded concerned and far more understanding than Walker would have been, considering the circumstances.

"You sure you didn't see or hear anything tonight?"

The man stopped on the stairs and stared over to her door, then his. "Like I said, walls are thin. Heard nothing except when she left. Can't believe someone could get in there without me hearing."

"Well, tell me about Kate. Any problems with her, anything unusual?"

The man was frowning. "Kate is quiet. Goes to work, comes home—sometimes plays that noisy rock stuff she listens to a little too loud, but she's a good kid. I've been a teacher a lot of years and would like to say I've seen it all, but tonight…" He actually laughed. "I hadn't."

The situation was far from funny, but Walker couldn't help himself from laughing along with the man. He was right. It had to have been a hell of a shock to open his door to a naked woman.

When Walker walked back into the neighbor's small apartment, almost identical in setup to Kate's, she appeared anxious as she searched him out.

"Well, anyone there?" she said.

He tossed her the blanket she'd dropped. "No, long gone."

"Great, so now what? What about the psycho chick who drove into the restaurant, can you arrest her?"

"No."

Obviously that wasn't what she wanted to hear, as she stood up so fast her towel slipped.

"Whoa!" one of the cops said as Walker caught a glimpse of her creamy white breast. It was even better than he'd pictured.

Walker took the blanket he was holding and wrapped it around her. "Here, before you lose what's left of that towel and give someone a heart attack."

"Well, I need to know why you can't arrest her," she snapped. "It's plain as day to me that Ryder's stalker did this. I mean, who else would do it? And how did she find out about me, anyway?"

"Well, that's a hell of a good question, considering you met this guy for the first time tonight. How many dates have you been on as of late? Could be any one of them with a possessive, jealous girlfriend. Or is there someone else, a married guy?" he asked.

"There is no one else—and I don't date married men!"

"Who did you last date? Let's start there."

She waved her hand and almost lost hold of the blanket.

"Just do us both a favor and keep your hands where they are," Walker said, interrupting her before she could start.

"What about that suit who came around a few times?" the elderly neighbor said from the doorway. They both turned toward him. Even the uniformed officer standing off to the side looked his way.

"What suit?" Walker asked, looking back at Kate.

She rolled her eyes again, and he was wondering if that was her way of trying to piss people off. Normally, when a woman did that, he found it annoying, but Kate was giving him ideas that could have gotten him arrested—namely the idea of having his hands on her and having her under him, naked, begging and pleading to let her come as he rammed into her over and over. She was trouble with a capital T, but he couldn't help but picture what his handprint on her creamy white backside would look like.

"Kate," he growled when she didn't answer.

"Todd Gray, a stockbroker. Thought he had possibility, but I discovered he had mother issues. I dumped him, haven't seen him since. Can't imagine a woman getting twisted up over the likes of him. He couldn't make a decision if his life depended on it. Had to consult his mother on everything." She shrugged. "Really, if a chick wants him, she can have him."

"Well, let's not rule him out." Walker turned to one of the officers and asked him to look into the guy. When Kate rattled off his number, he had to give her another look.

She shrugged again. "I have a great memory, good with numbers. I see it once, I don't forget." She glanced down at herself. "Look, I'd like to get some clothes on."

He looked down at her and her bare toes sticking out from under the blanket. "Well, for now your apartment is a crime scene. You can't go in. Besides, whoever did this, it would be a safe bet they could be back. Do you have someone you can call to stay with for the night?"

"Looking like this?" she spat. Then she held out her hand. "Can I use your phone?"

He pulled out his cellphone and handed it to her. "Make it fast," he said, and it earned him another of her frosty glares.

K ate could not believe this night. It was one of those nightmares that just seemed to go on and on, even though she was with that hot cop. She also needed to thank Mr. Harris. If it hadn't been for him, she was sure the detective would have had her sitting in his car naked, with only a blanket around her instead of the Seahawks sweatshirt Mr. Harris had dug out for her. Maybe he had agreed it wasn't okay that she couldn't go back into her own apartment and at least grab a robe— not that she remembered where she'd stuck it, in the closet or the laundry. But even a pair of jeans and shoes!

Here she was, still barefoot, sitting in the detective's car as he spoke to someone on his cellphone. There had to be some law against this. As far as she was concerned, she was tempted to push it.

Then there was her mother, whom she'd called and woken up. Added to that was the shock of hearing a man's voice in the background of the call: her dad's. Great, were they back together again, or was her mom just sleeping with him? She didn't want to go there, and she rubbed the bridge of her nose. There was a tap on her window, and she rolled it down. She couldn't remember the last time she'd been in a car with manual windows. Everything these days was electric.

"Yes?" she said to Detective Pruett.

"I thought you might like a pair of shoes." He not only handed her a pair of sneakers, the Reeboks she loved, but also a pair of jogging shorts and a tank top.

"Thank you. I thought you weren't going to let me have any clothes."

He was shaking his head, and his expression was pure mischief. Boy, talk about swallowing her heart. "No, I said you weren't going back in. I didn't say anything about me going in and getting you some clothes."

"So you ransacked my underwear drawers."

He was staring at her now with those deep green eyes, and she didn't know what to make of it. She unfastened her seatbelt and stepped into her shorts, pulling them on, not missing how his eyes flared when they rose up a bit. Then she bent over to slip her bare feet into her shoes. She heard him clear his throat, and she had to smile to herself. She put the tank top on the seat, as she was wearing Mr. Harris's sweatshirt. It covered her well, and she was warm, so she didn't feel the need to take it off in front of the detective.

"No, I found them in your front closet in a gym bag," he finally said. "Figured it was a safe bet."

"Sorry, I don't mean to be so—"

"A pain in the ass?"

"I'm not a pain in the ass! I just want what I want, and I didn't expect to have my life turned upside down tonight. I'm trying to meet someone nice and decent, not a loser. I mean, I'm a great catch, right?" she said. Maybe it was the way he was watching her, but she was starting to question everything, including herself. She ran her hand over her hair and wondered how she looked. Okay, why did he have to look so intense while he watched her? "What's wrong with me? Why are you looking at me like that?"

He was leaning in through the window, and he finally broke eye contact and glanced away. "So where am I taking you?" he said.

Talk about a change of subject. That worried her more. Maybe there was something wrong with her, and she was doomed to the same fate as her mother.

"To my mom's, which should be interesting, as my dad's there," she said. "I heard him in the background."

"And that's not a good thing?" he asked.

"No, it's not, considering my dad's cheated on my mom more times than I can count. My entire childhood was spent watching a revolving door of my dad leaving and coming back. They divorced five years ago, now…" She waved her hand and realized she was rambling again. "Sorry, I didn't mean to go on and on. I'm sure it sounds pretty pathetic, but I've got to tell you it helps that you at least brought me some shoes and shorts, as my parents are going to want some answers about why their only daughter is showing up half naked this time of night."

Why couldn't he say anything? It was becoming unnerving, the way he watched her.

"What is it?" she said. "Is there something in my hair? What's wrong with me? Why are you looking at me like that?" She ran her hands over her hair again.

"Kate, there's nothing wrong with you. You just

picked the wrong dude to try to get to know. Your parents, I don't know what to say. Your mom really keeps going back?"

She shrugged. What could she say? That was probably why her mom hadn't said anything to her, considering the last time her dad cheated and her mom left, Kate had sat her down for a heart to heart, asking if she had finally figured out that her and her dad would never work. "I'm not my mother," she said. She didn't know why she needed to say that, but she did.

He was about to say something when his cell phone rang. "Hold that thought." He stepped away from the car and barked, "Pruett."

She noticed the moment he stiffened and his expression changed, his eyes landing solely on Kate. The way he was watching her had the hair on the back of her neck prickling. Whatever was going on wasn't good, and it had to do with her.

"Well, why the hell would you let her go?" he snapped and turned away. She couldn't make out what else he said, and she went to open the car door and step out when he put his hand on the door and shut it again. Every part of his body language was tense—angry, too. From what she'd gathered from the little she knew of him, he was not a man anyone wanted to go up against.

"Shit." He pocketed his phone. "You stay in there," he snapped, pointing at her.

"Is everything all right?"

His hand was resting on the edge of the open window. He seemed to need a minute to collect himself. "The woman who drove through the restaurant, the one your date knew…well, she was just released."

For a second, Kate didn't know what to say, which

was unlike her. "Let me see if I have this right. Psycho bitch drives through the front of a restaurant, and you guys just let her go. What am I missing here? I'm not a detective, but I'm smart enough to realize that woman is a lunatic. Even you said she drove into that restaurant heading right for me." She could feel herself getting wound up.

"She claimed she lost control of the car, that she felt faint, that it was an accident. She had a lawyer show up, and we couldn't hold her. She's been charged with reckless endangerment and will have to appear before a judge in court tomorrow."

"Excuse me? She drove a car through a restaurant, which almost killed me, and wrecked a dress I spent a small fortune on, not to mention she wrote on my wall, which I'm now going to have to clean and possibly repaint—and I hate painting. She has two screws loose, and I'm the one being inconvenienced while you just let her go. What the hell is it with you—"

It happened so fast. His lips were on her, stopping her mid-sentence. If she'd wondered before whether Detective Pruett could kiss well, she didn't have to wonder anymore. This man knew how to kiss a woman, and she had no doubt he knew exactly what to do with one, as well. It was something she just knew when a man touched her. He was a man who'd need no instruction in the bedroom. She imagined, in that kiss, that it would be him directing her.

———

He told himself the kiss was only to shut her up, but he hadn't expected her to be so damn responsive. She matched his kiss, parting her lips so he could taste her as he held her head, running his teeth over her lower lip and sucking as she gasped. Then he caught himself and slowly let her lip go. She was breathing heavy—so was he—and the flickering heat in her eyes told him how much she wanted him. She was so damn responsive, and he imagined she would be like a wildfire in bed. He started to lean closer again, and she parted her lips when someone cleared his throat behind them.

He jumped and banged his head on the door. When he licked his lips, he could taste her on him, and something about it reminded him of peaches and cream. It was a summer fruit that he couldn't get enough of.

"What?" he snapped at the officer—Kramer, he thought his name was—who was standing there with a look of surprise. He even raised his eyebrows in humor. Of course he hadn't missed the fact that Walker had been kissing Kate, a woman who was the victim of a crime and the only interesting part of this entire bizarre night.

He didn't dare look down at Kate as he heard her sigh and then clear her throat. "And?" he added a little sharply when the officer said nothing, just looked from Kate back to him.

"Sorry," Kramer said. "The techs finished dusting for prints. They just scanned them in and got a match."

"So they know who was in my apartment," Kate said. The car door opened, and Walker held the edge of it as she slipped out. She brushed against him so close that he couldn't help letting his hand slip to her lower back.

The officer looked over at Walker. "It was Cindy Schmidt, the lady who drove through the restaurant."

"God dammit," Walker said. He wanted to punch something. He stepped back, jamming his fingers through his hair. Kate was watching him, looking to him for answers, for anything. She ran her hands over her elbows as if she needed to hold herself together. Shit, she now looked scared.

"How could she know about me?" she said. "I just met Ryder tonight. This isn't possible."

"I hate to tell you, Kate, but I've seen a lot of things. I'd like to say I've seen it all, but I haven't come close. Anything is possible—more than possible. You met him through online dating. You exchanged emails?"

She nodded. "We talked on the phone too, once, and then we met for a date, which was tonight."

"I want to know everything about Cindy: where she lives, what she does, even what she had for breakfast," he told Kramer. He watched the officer walk away to another squad car that had pulled up, and MacDonald climbed out.

"I'm not liking this too much," Kate said. "What's wrong with this chick? I mean, how pathetic can you be? A guy says no, go away. End of story. Move on. Have some pride, will you? And what the hell is wrong with him that he didn't see this? If he's being stalked by some psycho bitch, what the hell is he doing going online to look for more prey? I don't know who's worse, psycho babe or Ryder, who cheated on his wife with this woman. Do you know he stuck his profile up on the net when he was still married? I mean, what kind of guy does that? Creeps, that's who. It's almost as if he deserved getting saddled with a crazy woman who won't leave him alone."

He rested his hand on her shoulder, more to steady

her than anything, and she stopped talking. He could tell she was getting ready to lose it again. He was starting to recognize that when Kate got scared, she hid it with a bitchiness that could make his head spin, and she would go off on these tangents that could make a sane man crazy. But he saw it: it was all an act to cover up how terrified she was of a situation she had no control over.

"Oh my God, I have to work!" she said. "How am I going to get there? And I need my clothes. You know what? I'm done with psycho bitch. She's not chasing me out of here. I'm going up to my place and getting my clothes, and to hell with all of you." She pointed to her apartment building, and Walker could feel how tight she was. He had no doubt she was ready to race up there and scream at everyone to get out of her place.

"Stop!" he shouted at her.

She actually jumped, her eyes widened, but she didn't move a step from where she'd pulled away from him. She started pacing.

"You're scared, I get it, but stop being such a bitch about it. You can't go in, and until further notice, you can call in sick. Tomorrow, anyway. One day at a time, Kate."

"What? I can't miss work. I've worked so hard to get where I am. I've never missed a day. Just because I picked the wrong guy to go out with, why the hell am I being punished—"

"Kate." He touched her cheek, and she stopped. Maybe it was the way he spoke, so softly, that had her lip trembling. She was close to tears. Yeah, she was all bark. "It's going to be okay. Let's just get you out of here and off the street."

"Detective," MacDonald said, striding over to him.

"Kramer was just saying you wanted the background information on Cindy Schmidt. Well, I already did that. Thought it would be wise to know everything about her before she left, so I did some digging."

"And what did you find?"

"Well, you're not going to believe this. She's an IT tech—or was—for a pharmaceutical company here in Portland. She was let go after a harassment complaint was filed against her by a man who turned out to be her boss. She had somehow put a virus on his computer and had accessed his emails, all that shit. She was fired, signed a nondisclosure, and has been working as a programmer for some distributor." He looked up at Walker, but he didn't need to say it, as they both looked down at Kate.

"Where's your computer?" Walker asked.

"My MacBook? It's in my apartment, in the living room. Why?" But it only took her a second to figure out what he already knew. "He was hacked, and she tracked me through him," she said, pissed again. He could tell she wanted to kick something. "Son of a bitch!"

"Looks that way. Get her computer to the lab, and let's find out what else this Cindy knows about Kate," he said to MacDonald, who glanced at Kate and then nodded before going into her apartment building.

"All my personal information is on my computer. What am I supposed to do now?" she asked. "And how am I going to explain this to my mom and dad? Oh my God, what if she shows up at my mom's?"

She really was smart, too smart for her own good. He'd already thought of the same thing.

"You're not explaining anything," he said. "You're coming home with me."

CHAPTER

Ten

Going home with Detective Walker Pruett could have been one of the most exciting things she'd ever done if it weren't for the fact that she had a psychotic woman on her trail, a woman who had somehow figured that Kate was the one thing standing between her and Ryder Connelly—a man she didn't know, had met once, and wasn't dating! Kate hadn't argued with Walker about going with him, because the fact was that she felt much safer staying with the hunky detective than with her parents.

He parked outside an older two-story house with a small porch out front. It had a tree in the neat front yard and a lone straight-back chair sitting outside the front door. She followed him up the stairs in the dark and waited while he unlocked the door. It squeaked as he opened it and then flicked on a light. It was quaint. A sofa and chair and a sixty-inch flat-screen TV greeted her from the living room. A pool table was in the dining room instead of a table, and the art on the walls consisted of various Native pieces, completely clashing with this entire man-cave thing he had going on.

"So no missus here?" she asked, because it would have been just her luck.

The look he gave her answered that question. "Seriously, Kate?"

"Okay, just checking. With my track record, it wouldn't surprise me if you had some *Big Love* thing going on with a couple of sister wives." Now she was being ridiculous, she knew that, and she wondered what it was about Walker that made her say things she'd never say to anyone else.

"Do I look like the type of guy who has women stashed away? Good God, one woman is a handful. Now you think I have a harem."

"Sorry, my experience with men is somewhat jaded."

He grunted and allowed his gaze to linger on her breasts before meeting her eyes. "I'll show you the bathroom upstairs if you want to shower." He was already on the stairs, going up. If she didn't follow, she was pretty sure he was going to just leave her there, so she trotted after him, up the stairs, until she was right behind him. He didn't look back, though. "I'll get you a T-shirt to sleep in, and you can take my bed." He was giving orders suddenly, so cold, changing from a man who'd stopped her with one of the most breathtakingly hot kisses she had ever had to a man who was all business, who couldn't get away from her fast enough. What had she done now?

The stairs squeaked. She figured the house had to be sixty years old, give or take a decade or two. It had dark wood and white walls. Even the floorboards creaked when she walked. The bathroom was dated but surprisingly clean, for a guy.

"There're extra towels in the cupboard in the bathroom." He pointed at the door as if giving a tour and kept walking.

She followed on his heels, past one of the two bedrooms upstairs. The first door was open and had boxes on the desk and other junk piled in it.

"And this is my bedroom," he said. It was small and had a four-poster bed, neatly made, covered in a dark blue quilt, with one pillow. He opened a chest of drawers and pulled out a white shirt. She didn't miss how neatly folded his shirts were—a far cry from hers. Most things were jammed in her drawers, and she could barely close them.

"Wow, it's surprisingly clean. I would have expected something not so neat."

He gave her an odd look, the expression on his face almost unreadable. "Really, you mean like the trail you left at your place? First your red dress—which, by the way, is a work of art on you—then your lacy black bra and underwear. What did you do, step out of everything and drop them as you walked to your bedroom?"

How had he known? She swallowed, because that was exactly what she'd done. She gripped his T-shirt closer, feeling her bare nipples brush the inside of the sweatshirt. Even though she was wearing shorts, as well, she felt absolutely naked in front of him. And, right now, she didn't want to be anywhere else.

He was so close to her, and he made no attempt to move back or away. Seemed to her he really enjoyed invading her space. There was something about the way a man smelled when she was attracted to him that was better than hot fudge—and she loved fudge, anything chocolate, deep and sweet and rich. He raised an eyebrow when she didn't answer.

"Okay, so I'm not the neatest," she said. "Can I just say, in my defense, I was on my way to take a shower?"

The way his gaze drifted down over the bulky sweatshirt she was wearing to her bare legs and then lower, taking in all of her, was the most intimate gesture she'd ever experienced. She had to squeeze her legs together. Good God, what would it be like to have this man fuck her? She had no doubt he'd know how to do it right—and no doubt she'd think she'd died and gone to heaven. He gazed at her lower lip as she slipped her tongue out and over it. She wanted him to lean in and taste her, kiss her hard and fast and deep as he did.

Then he had her pressed against the wall, her arms above her head, and he held them with one hand in a grip she knew she couldn't get away from, not that she wanted to move one inch from this man. No, she wanted him closer, feeling every hard inch of him pressed into her. She heard a sound and realized it was her. She'd whimpered.

"You want me hard and fast or tender and easy? Come on, Kate. Tell me what you want," he said. He slipped his leg in between hers, and he was thick and long, pressing into her. His breath was warm as he stared so close, his eyelids heavy, eyes filled with desire. Yeah, he wanted her too.

He slipped his hand under her sweatshirt, sliding it up over her stomach, taking his time feeling her curves. His fingers skimmed the underside of her breast, tracing the line left from the elastic of her bra and then around her nipple, his thumb brushing over the hard peak. Her knees started to buckle. If he hadn't been pressed against her, his leg between hers, she'd have fallen to the floor. At the friction of his leg against her, pressing into her core, she rubbed against him on instinct. His hand, his thumb—she exploded against him. The orgasm was mind blowing, and it went on and on as he continued to press his thigh into her, pulling now on her nipple.

He still hadn't kissed her.

He was holding her hands above her head and watching with a satisfied grin. "Tell me, was that as hot for you as it was for me?"

She didn't think she could speak. She felt completely open for him even though she still was dressed. She felt as if he had access to all of her. She whimpered again, and he leaned closer. He didn't kiss her lips, but he was so close she could almost touch hers to his. He wouldn't let her, though, as he angled his head and smiled seductively.

"Tell me, Kate, what do you want?"

Would he tease her endlessly until she told him? Did he want her to beg? "I want your hands on me. I want you to touch me."

"Do you want me to fuck you too?"

She did, more than anything. Did that make her naughty, a bad girl who was supposed to make love, not fuck? "It's such a bad word."

He brushed his nose lightly to hers, his lips touching her cheek. "It is what it is, Kate. Don't start calling it something it's not. If it's sex, hot and dirty, you call it that. Answer me. What do you want? You need to say the words, or this is as far as this goes." His lips brushed her cheek, her ear, and lower, to her jaw. He nipped at her ear.

"Walker, I want you to fuck me, hard, and don't stop —please."

His one hand gripped her wrists, and his other framed her chin, holding her still. He kissed her hard, his tongue invading her mouth, tasting her. He was taking, but she'd given him the okay, and he was going to handle her, it seemed, his way. This was going to happen. There wasn't a chance she'd be able to reason soon just being in the vicinity of him, and right now she couldn't think even if she wanted to. She'd never been with a man who handled things, but this man wasn't only confident: she knew without a doubt this would be done his way and with him in charge.

Then her hands were free as he lifted her sweatshirt and tossed it. He didn't take her hands again. No, this time he put his hands on both breasts, cupping, caressing, touching, and then he lifted her, and her legs went around his waist as he slid his hand over her rounded cheeks, holding her to him as he lay her on the bed. He reached for her foot and pulled off one shoe, then the other. They clunked to the floor, and he was still in his jacket, fully dressed, though she was already half naked. He watched her, his gaze absolutely sizzling, as he slipped off his coat and unclipped his gun from his belt, setting it inside a drawer beside the bed.

He was fast, the way he reached out and pulled off her shorts. She didn't think she could go another second without touching him, so she went up on her knees on the bed as he moved toward her. She slid her hand over his cheek, the light beard he'd started to grow. She didn't think she'd like a man with a beard, but Walker's wasn't heavy. It was light and soft and made his lips fuller, more kissable, if that was possible.

She started to unbutton his shirt between kissing him. His hand was roaming freely down her back and over her curvy butt. He took his time, feeling her curves and then between her legs to feel how wet she was. God, she could take him now and she'd die a happy woman.

She opened his shirt, and he had the most amazing chest. There was a light covering of hair over amazing pecs, and, getting a firsthand look at his arms, she pushed off his shirt. Yeah, he was strong, but she'd already felt that.

He already had his belt undone, and he slipped off his pants. He was as naked as her, pushing her back on the bed, crawling above her. He was so ready for her, and although she'd felt his size pressed against her, seeing him in his full glory, there wasn't a chance she wasn't going to be satisfied.

He slid his hand between her legs and then touched her thigh, sliding his fingers up the inside of her soft skin, pushing her knee up and open to him. He was watching her, maybe giving her one more chance to say no—or maybe not, as he pressed a kiss to the back of her knee while watching her reaction.

She reached out and touched him, sliding her hand around him, feeling the size of him.

"Easy, baby," he said, his voice a hiss. Then he rolled on his back, taking her with him. She was holding him and straddled over him, and she leaned down and kissed his chest, allowing her tongue to trace over his nipples. What would it be like to just slide down and take him in her mouth?

He had his hands on her breasts again, playing, twisting her nipples. Then he flipped her over so fast that she was on her hands and knees, and he was reaching into the bedside drawer. She heard him rip open a condom and slip it on.

"Walker, I want to touch you," she said as he started to fill her, and she dropped her head as she felt every inch of him slide in. He was so big.

"No, you need to hang on," he said, and he started rocking her hard. Her back was pressed to his chest, and he slid his arm around her hips to hold her tight. She couldn't help the squeal that slipped out. Oh my God, could this man fuck. It was such a turn on, feeling him skin to skin, holding her so she couldn't move and was completely at his mercy. This man should have come with a warning, she realized, as he filled her over and over.

The bed frame banged the wall, and she slapped her palm to the bedpost to hold on as the man completely sent her over the edge. She swore she saw stars when she completely lost control. She vaguely heard herself screaming, shouting his name as she clawed at his hand, his other holding her, kissing her shoulder as her entire body trembled over and over. Then he growled and swore, pounding into her harder and faster, when all she wanted was to fall down on the bed and not move, but he held her up while he finished.

Then he collapsed with her onto the bed.

Eleven

H e'd died and gone to heaven.

Then the cold reality bit him as he stared at the naked woman—who had the curviest ass he'd ever seen in his twenty-eight years—next to him. Kate was lying on his bed, and her breathing was light. He wondered if, in fact, she'd fallen asleep. What the fuck was he thinking, screwing a woman he should be protecting? He didn't even want to think about all the ethical boundaries he'd just crossed. He ripped off the condom and walked across the hall to the bathroom to dump it in the garbage. When he strode back into the bedroom, the bedside light was on, and Kate had crawled under the comforter.

He stood before her, naked, and she sat up, running her gaze over him. She wasn't shy, and he could tell she appreciated what she saw. But then…hell, look at her! She had a pair of tits that could make a man howl, and her ass gave him enough to hang on to. She wasn't a toothpick, she was a woman: curvy enough, strong enough that she could take him and keep up with him.

He didn't want to worry about a woman breaking under him.

There were times like now when he just wanted to ride a woman hard. It was satisfying. He didn't want soft and easy. His life wasn't made that way. He wasn't made that way.

"No regrets," he said to her. He didn't ask, because the last thing he wanted was a woman having second thoughts after all was done.

"None, you?" she asked him, sliding her knees up and wrapping her arms around them.

He could smell her from where he was, and he felt himself hardening again. There were times when he could walk away satisfied after having a woman, but there was something about Kate and the way she watched him, so seductive and sensual, that stirred something in him. She wasn't asking for a commitment. She had offered him her body, and he had taken it.

He shook his head and grabbed the corner of the comforter to rip it back. She squealed again, and her breasts bounced as she jumped. He found himself wanting to taste them, and he climbed onto the bed as she lay back and across it. He crawled over her, holding himself up as he took in her expression of awe. There was passion in this woman that had been buried beneath layers of complexity. Right now, he felt as if he'd peeled one back. How many more layers did this woman have?

He ran his tongue over her nipple and then took it in his mouth and sucked. She pressed her head back into the bed and gasped. Her hands, she didn't know what to do with them, so she rested them beside her head.

"I wonder if I can make you come apart just from touching you like this," he said, and he ran his tongue over her nipple again. She hissed, her hands in his hair. Yes, she was trying to gain control, he could feel it in her, so he took her hands and pressed them above her head, rising up over her. She moved those amazing hips, trying to gain some release. He could see how she was building up to a frenzy, all because he'd taken her control away. He wondered if she ever let go. Probably not, but tonight she was going to. He'd make damn sure of it.

Twelve

She wasn't sure she could move. As the warm water ran over her back and down the drain, she pressed her cheek to the tile and closed her eyes. She heard him climb in behind her, and his hand slid up over her stomach and moved in circles. How could just a single touch from Walker have her ready again? She wanted him just like the last time, when he'd rolled over on his back and slid her on top so she could ride him. Walker had controlled every moment of her time on top. He had energy and then some. It couldn't be possible for her to want him again like this, and she feared tomorrow she'd be mighty sore.

"Good God, you're amazing," he said as he pressed against her, kissing her shoulder and running his hand over her supersensitive breasts. She didn't think there was a part of her this man hadn't touched. "You're insatiable." He kissed her again.

"Me? You. I'm so tired," she murmured. Tired and sated. She didn't think there was a tense bone left in her body after Walker made love to her six times. No, he hadn't made love. He'd screwed her, hard. They'd been like animals, but he was ever so good and demanding. She hadn't known she had it in her to respond that way to a man, this man who was like no one she'd ever met. No man had ever made love—correction, fucked her like this.

"No one has inspired me like you," he said.

She turned around in the water and slipped her arms over his shoulders to gaze up at him. "Really?" What was it about this man that made her think this was something she'd like to explore?

He leaned in and kissed her again. Her lips felt bruised and used, and she still wanted more. He lifted her against the tile, her back pressed to the hard surface. How could he be ready again? He slipped inside her. He was wet and oh, so sexy. Her breasts brushed the hair on his chest. She hung on to him as he pushed her legs wide and moved inside her. He wasn't fast or hurried this time. He made a point of her knowing who she was with. He watched her expression, her response to him as he moved inside her and then stayed there. She touched his face, running her thumb over his lip, and he nipped the side of it with his teeth. She'd never felt so close to a man before. How was it possible? She wondered if this was what happened to women after a one-night stand. But then, after a night of sex like this with Walker, she didn't want it to end.

He was inside her so deeply, her legs wrapped around him as he suddenly stopped and rested his head against hers. "I forgot a condom. This is what you do to me."

She wanted to cry, because she didn't want him to

pull out, so she tightened her legs around him when he tried to pull away.

"Come on, Kate. I can't hold on much longer." He touched her lips with his.

"It's okay, I'm on the pill," she whispered, even though she didn't know him and it wasn't smart. But right now, she didn't care.

He slid his hand over her bottom and held her there. "This isn't wise, you know. I can't—there're diseases, and you don't know me. I don't know you."

Maybe he was right, but he still didn't pull out. He stayed inside her. She didn't mean to kiss him again. She just touched his lips, tasting him, and he slid his hands up her back before lifting her off.

"Oh my God, stay there," he said. "I'll be right back."

He left her cold in a warm shower, wanting to weep, but he was back a moment later, covering himself, water spilling out of the shower onto the floor, and he lifted her, pressing her back to the tile, and drove into her hard and fast. It was only seconds later that she was screaming his name.

"Walker, you up there?" There was a shout from downstairs, a woman's voice.

He groaned, still inside her. "Oh shit," he muttered and pulled out. There was no just being together, no being satisfied and wrung out, no clinging to each other as they tried to return to reality.

"Who is that?" she asked. She was still holding on to him, and his arms stayed around her, sliding her down his body until she was standing on shaky legs. Her brain started to comprehend the sound: a woman calling for

Walker in his house while Kate was upstairs screwing his brains out.

"Kruso" was all he said as he turned off the shower, stepped out, grabbed a towel, and wrapped it around his waist. Kate stepped out and reached for a towel hanging on the hook, feeling very much the other woman. And here he was, acting so cavalier.

Kate was freaking out over the woman's voice. She was coming up the stairs. "Is it your wife?" she said. Of course it had to be. It would be just her luck.

He turned his head slowly and stopped drying himself off with an expression that had her shutting her mouth. "Seriously?" he said. "After that, you still think I have a wife?" He pulled open the door and didn't give her a chance to say a word.

"Hey, you didn't answer your phone," the mystery woman said. "Listen, we have a problem."

Kate pulled the towel up, her hair dripping, as she stared at the short, plump redhead outside the bathroom.

"What is it?" Walker said, stepping to the side to block the door so Red couldn't see her. Maybe he wasn't such a jerk after all.

"Sorry, didn't mean to interrupt," Red said, "but I thought you should know we got a 911 call come in from Ryder Connelly. Someone trashed his place. Units are on the way over there."

Walker glanced back at Kate. Even with water dripping from him, the man looked like a god. She stepped closer, resting her hand on his shoulder as he glanced back at her. She stood right behind him. He didn't say anything, but there was something in the exchange, and she didn't miss the interest from the short redhead watching them. It was a look filled with amusement.

"Kruso, this is Kate," Walker said, gesturing between them before setting both hands on his hips. Kate actually stuck her hand out through the V in Walker's arm, reaching around.

Kruso shook her hand. "Nice to meet you, Kate. Saw you at the station earlier."

When the towel slipped, Kate pulled her hand back to cover herself again. "Nice to meet you too," she said, moving closer behind Walker and looking over his shoulder. "Awkward," she said.

"Yeah, listen, why don't I wait downstairs?" Kruso said. She glanced down at Walker's towel hanging low on his hips and raised her eyebrows. "…And give you a chance to get dressed?" She looked around Walker again. "Sorry to interrupt."

Kate was dripping, her ass hanging out of the towel. "Is she your partner?" she said.

"Walker doesn't have a partner, Kate," Kruso called up the stairs, obviously having overheard. "He's the lone wolf, doesn't work well with others."

"Hey, that's not true. I can work with anyone," he shouted after her.

"Only if they're doing it your way," she shouted back.

"You're a pain in the ass, Kruso. It's amazing your husband and kids put up with you."

Kate could hear the detective laughing just as Walker reached for her hand and dragged her across the hall back into the bedroom and shut the door.

She was still dripping. The bedside light showed the crumpled mess of the bed. She ran the towel over herself and then dried the ends of her hair. Walker was pulling on jeans and a clean T-shirt. She didn't miss the fact that he'd omitted any underwear.

"Here." He handed her a dark blue T-shirt. "Put this on and meet me downstairs."

Kate took the shirt and pulled it on. "You seen my shorts?" She was bending over, lifting Walker's dress pants from the floor, when she spied her gray running shorts and felt the light smack on her bare bottom.

She jumped up. "Hey!" Her hand touched the spot his had landed on.

"You have a great ass," he said, and he pulled open the door and walked out.

Kate stood there, listening as the man who'd had her in every way imaginable jogged down the stairs, whistling.

B y the time Walker arrived downstairs, Kruso had already helped herself to a soda. The thing of it was that there wasn't a detective he worked with who hadn't shown up here when he was home. Most knocked before walking right in. Kruso, although an anomaly among the bigger cops around her, fit in kind of like the team mascot. She was tough, foulmouthed, and smart, and her youngest kid was just out of diapers.

"So when did you start bringing witnesses and victims of crimes home and sleeping with them?" she asked before taking a swallow of ginger ale.

"When did you start just walking into my place?"

She shrugged. "I knocked, you didn't answer. I got worried, is all." She jutted her chin toward the stairs. "So?" she asked, waiting him out.

"She's interesting" was all he could say. The truth was that Kate had kind of bowled him over. The sizzle between them was off the charts, and he'd never experienced a woman like her. He'd thought that after the first time, he'd be satisfied, but he still wasn't, not by a long shot. It was the taste of her, and every time he had her, he wanted more.

"Hmm," she said.

He wasn't sure he liked the way Kruso was eyeing him up. Before she could start poking her nose in his business any more, he decided to steer the conversation away from his libido. "So what happened with this Ryder dude? You said he called 911."

"Units are on their way, should be there now. Apparently his place was trashed. That's all I know. Thought you wanted to know, as well, since this is your case—and you are, after all, protecting the victim."

The way she said it, Walker knew she was trying to get the conversation back on Kate. "What about Cindy Schmidt? Where is she?"

Kruso was wearing the same tweed jacket she always did, with dark pants. Her cropped hair looked as if she'd gotten out of bed in a hurry and forgotten to brush it. "Well, that's the thing. She's not at home. We've got units out looking for her. The crime lab had a go at your Kate's computer and found a virus on it."

He heard the creak on his stairs and turned to see Kate in his T-shirt and her shorts, still barefoot, her wet hair combed back. She had a killer body and stirred his interest more than a woman ever had. Talk about a match in bed!

"A virus on my computer?" she asked. "How can that be? I have an antivirus program on there that's supposed to be top notch and catch everything."

Kruso gave her a look, taking in her attire. "Well, that's the thing. Nothing can protect you from every-thing, and as soon as an antivirus program has a patch to catch a virus or other malware on your computer, more are created that slip through."

"Great. That's just great," Kate added, sounding annoyed.

Walker could understand, to a point. He held out his hand, and Kate took it, stepping beside him. Of course Kruso didn't miss the gesture. "So her computer has a virus. What does that have to do with Cindy, the IT gal stalking Ryder Connelly?"

"It means that someone put a virus on my computer, hacked into it, and has my information," Kate said. "Am I not correct, Detective? I assume you know who did it, too."

He wondered for a minute whether Kate was going to ramble on again. Good God, she was so outspoken, but he was also starting to realize she wasn't just a woman with a pair of breasts to die for, killer curves, and long legs that wrapped around him and held on while he drove into her. She was smart.

"You're right," Kruso said. "It appears that someone has been watching everything you've done. We've had trouble tracing it back, but crime lab did. Whoever did it is good, but we're better. And Ms. Cindy Schmidt has been watching you, reading your emails. She most likely has the same virus on Ryder Connelly's computer. It just happened you were the one he was in contact with."

"So that's how she knew I was meeting Ryder for dinner. She planned that little drive through." Kate was squeezing his hand, but if he hadn't been holding it, he never would have known she was trembling. It was so subtle, and now he knew how truly scared she was. She was good at hiding her feelings, but he was getting better at reading her. The body never lied, and Kate's sure as hell didn't.

"Well, let's get on over to Ryder Connelly's and see what's going on," Walker said.

"Great, I'll get my shoes." Kate pulled away, starting for the stairs.

"Wait!" he snapped. "You're not going anywhere."

"What? Of course I am," Kate said, and he could tell she was ready to argue, so he started toward her.

"No, you're staying here, where I know you'll be safe. I'm going to a crime scene. You're not coming." He stepped closer, putting his hands on the finest ass he'd ever seen. "Go get in bed, and wait for me there."

The flicker of heat in her eyes was enough to make his jeans feel tight and damn uncomfortable, but she leaned in and kissed him, then turned and started up the steps, flicking him a heated look that had him wanting nothing more than to follow her upstairs and sate his desire.

"Smooth there, Walker," Kruso said. "Maybe you want to go tie her to your bed before we leave."

He turned to Kruso, who smiled innocently. "She's not coming," he said, jamming his feet into his shoes and grabbing his leather jacket from the back of the sofa.

"Maybe not right now."

"Good God, you've got a dirty mind." He grabbed the front door and ripped it open. "Let's go," he said as Kruso followed, laughing softly.

R yder Connelly lived in an upscale condo in downtown Portland: two bedrooms, a view to die for, tastefully decorated in blues and greens. Everything was modern, new, and expensive, including the chef's open kitchen, which, in Walker's opinion, was far too neat for a single man. It was, in fact, the only room in the house left untouched by whoever had trashed the place.

Two uniformed officers were there, taking Ryder's statement, when Walker arrived with Kruso. By his last glance at his watch, it was 4:10 a.m.

"Whoever was here didn't like him very much," Kruso said, snapping on a pair of gloves.

Walker pulled a pair of latex gloves from his coat pocket and snapped them on, as well, though he preferred to be by himself when taking in a scene. At times, he could almost picture what was going through the perp's head, what had driven them to do what they'd done.

CHEATER was painted across what looked like a

really ugly expensive painting. HATE YOU, FRAUD, DIRTY DOG, SUFFER, and then it was as if someone had taken a butcher knife over the leather grain sofa, the stuffing pulled out. Such a waste. In the master bedroom, the king-size bed had been slashed, as well, the bedding ripped and shredded. Feathers from the torn pillows filled the room.

"Wow, someone did *not* like him." Kruso was behind him and walking through the room. "Look at the clothes in the closet. It looks like someone cut all his pants to make them shorter."

Walker watched as Kruso picked up a pile of material scattered all over the floor. "Not just making a mess, this is personal. Someone really hates him," he said.

"Why cut up every one of his pants to make them too short?"

"To piss him off, is my guess. Slick out there seems pretty stylish. Would think this would get to him. This is someone who's really angry with him," he added, walking into the bathroom and taking in the mess. He didn't know why, but he picked up the shampoo bottle and took a whiff as he unscrewed it. "Shit! Acid," he said. He put the bottle back and started back out. He spotted a crime scene tech coming in, wearing a dark jacket and gloves. "Hey, go through this bathroom," he told her. "Bet you some of these containers have been swapped out. There's acid in the shampoo. Whoever did this wanted to really hurt this guy. This is personal."

There was something about this vandalism that just didn't feel right, and it wasn't anything he could put his finger on right now. He walked out into the dining area, where floor-to-ceiling windows made up the one wall that gave this condo a million-dollar view. Ryder was pacing like a mad man, furious as he spoke to the cops.

"I want her arrested!" He started toward Walker, his fists clenched as if ready to punch something, angry as all hell.

"We don't know yet that it was her," Walker said. "We'll dust for prints. I'd like to know how she got in. There are no signs of a break and enter, and that lock is clean. Cindy ever been here?"

Ryder crossed his arms and stared at him. "No, I was still living with my wife when we hooked up." The man didn't say anything else but appeared shamed. This was the kind of thing that ate away at people.

"Tell me again where you met her," Walker said, because he'd read the report. The guy had put up a profile on a dating site, looking for casual sex, and had been answered by this Cindy. He'd never said he was married, just not looking for a commitment. Met her at a bar, had some drinks, and then had sex.

"I told you already: online. She wanted to meet me, no strings, just sex. It was great until after, and then it felt like crap."

"So where did you meet up? Her place, hotel, where?"

Ryder wiped around his mouth. Man, did he look uncomfortable. "My wife was away at her sister's with the baby and our older daughter. I took Cindy to my place."

Walker wondered whether Slick had ever figured out how stupid that was. "So you brought a strange woman home to your house while your wife and children were away and did her in the bed you share with your wife."

Ryder Connelly had the good grace, at least, to

blush. Walker was no saint, but he knew you never brought another woman into your wife's bed. It seemed so skanky.

"If I could go back and undo a lot of things, I would," Ryder said. "But I can't. All I can say in my defense is that it was a huge lapse in judgement on my part."

Stupid idiot was what crossed Walker's mind. "Hmm," he said and looked around again. "So who else has a key to this place?"

Ryder was shaking his head. "Management, cleaning lady, my sister—my wife," he said.

"You're married and still went out on a date?" Walker said. He was really pissed that this jerk had done that to Kate. Not that this guy was ever going to get within ten feet of Kate again, but it still pissed him off that she had been tricked by him.

"Sorry, old habit. My ex-wife. We're divorced," he said, but Walker could tell he wished that wasn't the way it was.

"I've just got to ask. Why Kate?" he asked.

The man looked at him for a moment, confused. "Who?"

"Seriously, dude?" Walker laughed, but he wasn't amused. Kate would have been just another notch on this man's bedpost.

"Walker!" Kruso called out. He turned to see her hurrying from the bedroom, holding a red notebook in her hand. "Found it under the mattress. Read this."

"Hey, that's not mine," Ryder said, sounding defensive.

Walker took the small lined book and read a handwritten entry: "Kill Kate." He glanced up at Ryder, who read the words, and his face paled. He raised his hands in defense, walking backward.

"No, no, that's not mine. That's not even my writing." He was freaking out, and an officer put a hand on his shoulder. He swung back his arm to brush him off. Bad move. In the next second, Ryder was on the ground, face digging into the carpet, and cuffed.

Walker was already on his way to the front door. "Kruso!" he yelled, then caught the keys in midair.

"Go!" was all she said.

Walker was out the door.

Fifteen

She was having the most delicious erotic dream. She was sweaty and couldn't move a muscle in her body after her most mind-blowing orgasm yet. Walker was amazing. Did that man know how to touch her, how to love her—no, fuck her, she had to remind herself.

She heard a noise and blinked, turning to the bedside clock in the darkened bedroom. It took her a moment to remember she was in Walker's bedroom, in his bed, and her body ached. She needed him again.

She heard a noise again from downstairs and smiled as she realized Walker was back. She couldn't wait to touch him, and she had plans of going down on him, taking him into her mouth. Maybe she'd have him begging her. She licked her lips in anticipation as she waited for him to start up the stairs, and still there was nothing.

"Walker," she called out.

He didn't answer, so she slid back the quilt, slipped her bare legs over the side, and stood up naked. She'd felt so naughty as she slipped into bed with nothing on.

There was something about being skin to skin with nothing between her and Walker that seemed so bad and so right. Sex with Walker, on a scale of one to ten, was a two hundred. It was mind blowing, amazing, and she didn't want it to end.

She started to the top of the darkened stairs and stared down into darkness. Then she wondered for a minute about pulling on one of his t-shirts, but she smiled as she thought of greeting him with not a stitch on—maybe testing out the pool table downstairs. She started down the stairs, seeing a light coming from the kitchen. Maybe he hadn't heard her as she walked down the stairs, each step creaking as loud as the next.

"Walker," she called out again. Then she heard a rattle from the kitchen. She stopped on the last step, waiting for him to appear, but there was nothing. "What the heck?" she said, wondering why he wasn't answering.

She was shivering now, wishing she'd pulled on a shirt, something, and at the same time thinking maybe he was having second thoughts about her being there. It would be a horrible loss, and she hoped he wasn't the type. At the same time, because of all her past failures, she feared that maybe, in fact, he was. She crossed her arms over her breasts as she stepped off the last step and started into the kitchen. The light was bright in the small walk through, a couple of empty beer bottles on the counter, a soda can with them, a bag of Doritos opened with a few chips spilling out.

But no Walker.

"Walker, what's going on?" she called out louder, listening to a creak on the stairs and then footsteps going up. She stopped and walked over to the stairs, listening.

Was he mad at her? Did he want her to leave? Damn prickly man. She started back up the stairs, her pride taking a hammering.

"Walker, you know what? I'm so done with guys treating me like crap. I don't know what's going on with you and what bug you've got shoved so far up your ass right now—" She stopped in the doorway of the bedroom.

The bedside light was on, but it was the steel knife held by a woman dressed in black tights and a hoodie that had her freezing for what felt like forever before she could grab a breath and scream.

CHAPTER
Sixteen

He heard the scream from outside as he jumped out of Kruso's small white compact. His hand was at his waist, pulling his sidearm from the holster. He flicked the safety as he ran up the steps and opened the front door.

"Kate!" he yelled as the front door crashed against the wall. He stepped inside, looking right and left, taking in everything, from the light on in the kitchen to the darkened stairs, all in a split second. There was no one, nothing, and all he could hear was his heart hammering in his chest.

"Kate, you answer me right now!" he yelled.

He heard crying. "Walker!" she called out, and damn if she didn't sound scared—no, terrified.

"Where are you, Kate?" He was walking in, his arm out, his stance all cop, ready to fire as he cleared the entry, the doorway to the kitchen. His back to the wall, looking up, he could hear Kate crying, then another voice he couldn't make out. He was almost to the stairs and flicked on the light behind him, lighting up the living room and the dining area, where the pool table was. He was pointing his gun, looking around the corner. Nothing, no one.

He stepped on the first stair and looked up to a silhouette. It was Kate, naked, with a knife to her throat and what looked like a woman behind her. He couldn't see her face. She was hiding behind Kate.

"Kate, are you okay, baby?" he called out rather sharply.

"Walker, help me," she whispered.

He could see the fear in her eyes. "Hey, put the knife down and move away from her—now!" he shouted, taking another step up carefully, his gun pointed just off to Kate's right. But whoever it was had no intention of dropping the knife, as she pressed it harder to Kate's throat. Kate gasped, and a drop of blood appeared. Her fingers scraped and clawed at the woman's wrist in panic.

"Okay, okay, just calm down!" Walker said. "Don't do anything stupid. Don't hurt her. What is it you want? Just tell me!" He was freaking out and so close to losing it. For the first time, his hand was shaking on his gun. That wasn't him, he was always the steady one, but right now the thought of watching this crazy person slit Kate's throat was making him lose the ability to function.

"Cindy, it's not going to end like this," he said. "Just put the knife down, and we'll talk. Kate isn't interested in Ryder. She's with me. She's in my house, waiting for me." He was trying to think of anything he could to reason with this crazy person. Why wasn't she answering? She just stood there. The look in Kate's eyes, the expression on her face, was trying to tell him something, but he just couldn't figure out what it was. He could hear sirens in the background, coming closer, but he feared backup would come too late.

He stared at Kate, trying to reassure her. The way she pleaded with him, those amazing hazel eyes that reflected the color of amber in the glistening tears that now popped in her eyes. He didn't want to see the life drain out of them. "Cindy, this isn't the way to handle this! Let Kate go now. She's done nothing to you."

Kate gave a slight shake of her head. For a moment, he thought it was just fear, but then he realized she really was trying to say something. He stared hard at her as she opened her mouth, gasping. "Not…C—cindy," she stuttered.

"Walker, behind you," someone whispered.

He didn't look, but he could hear the officers coming in. Kruso was there too. "She's at the top of the stairs with a knife to Kate's throat," he said. He didn't dare look over to the door. He was afraid to look away, scared that Kate wouldn't be there when he looked back. "I'm going to take another step up," he said more loudly. "Who are you? Just tell me what you want, and I'll make sure you get it."

"Don't!" The woman finally spoke, and Kate shut her eyes. "She has to die. He'll just call her again. He'll sleep with her. It's what he does."

"Who does? Who are we talking about?" He moved his foot to take another step, and the wood creaked.

Then Kate elbowed her in the stomach, and the woman pushed her forward. Time froze. He saw the shock as Kate's arms flew up. She lost her footing on the first step and fell, naked. When she hit the first step, he took everything in: the woman had long hair in a ponytail. He fired his gun, missing her by an inch, splintering the wood in the wall by her head. She ducked, and Kate was rolling, trying to grab hold of a post to stop her fall. He heard another shot from upstairs as he reached Kate, and he looked up as the woman slid against the wall, down to the floor. The smear of blood stained his white wall as she fell.

"Kate, are you okay?" He was kneeling beside her, his gun in his hand, and she slid up, brushing her hair from her eyes, holding her wrist.

"Walker, I thought she was you. I heard a noise downstairs, and I came down, but it was her in the house."

He was touching her, and he glanced up the stairs to Kruso, who was beside the woman. A small branch was sticking from her short red hair, and she was breathing heavy, kicking the knife away and pulling her cuffs from her back pocket. "Shoulder wound," she said. "Call EMS."

The woman screamed as Kruso rolled her over and cuffed her hands behind her back.

"Oh my," Walker heard someone mutter behind him, and he glanced back to see MacDonald eyeing up Kate's nakedness. He didn't miss the appreciation as the man took in her breasts. They were, in fact, a work of art.

Walker slipped off his coat and put it around Kate's shoulders as he sat beside her on the step. "You scared me," he said. She was shaking as she leaned against him. There was something about having this woman in his arms that felt so right, and he realized that without her here, he would feel empty.

"Walker?" she asked. "Do you think I could get my clothes?"

He laughed. "Yeah, I'll get you some."

When he glanced up the stairs at Kruso, she was giving him the thumbs up. It was then that he noticed the tear in her jacket as she holstered her gun, her hand on her hip. "How the hell did you get up there?" he asked, taking in the short woman, who was assessing the suspect bleeding at her feet.

"I climbed the tree outside your window," she said. "You really should get a lock on there. And, jeez, get some clothes on your girlfriend."

He wasn't sure who stiffened first, him or Kate. Girlfriend? When he looked back up at Kruso, the sly bugger was leaning on the rail, grinning.

"Are you sure?" Walker was in the emergency room, waiting just outside the curtained-off area.

Kruso was looking up at him, the top of her head barely reaching his shoulders. "She's Ryder's ex-wife. I know, I can't believe it, either. Andrea Connelly broke into your house to kill Kate."

"Is she out of surgery yet?"

"Yeah, it was just a shoulder wound through and through. They cleaned it and stitched her up." She looked up at Walker. "Just in case you're wondering, I always hit where I aim."

He wondered, for a minute, whether she was referring to the fact that he'd missed. "I'm sure you do. Did they find Cindy?"

She nodded. "It's a shame. This whole thing didn't have to happen."

He didn't miss the moment he spotted Ryder racing to the nurses' station. He looked frantic and pretty rough, as if he'd just gotten out of bed and pulled on the first thing he could find. He was very upset, and although Walker couldn't make out what he was saying, he could hear enough. The man was beside himself.

"Look who just walked in," Kruso said. She looked over at the distraught man. "Cindy was tucked into Mrs. Connelly's trunk—stabbed, her throat slit."

The curtain popped open, and the doctor walked out. The young intern stopped and gestured behind himself. "She's good to go any time. We've got her papers signed," he said.

"Thank you," Walker said as he looked over at Kate, who was lying on the bed, a bandage over the cut on her neck, her wrist wrapped. Her chin was still scraped from earlier that night.

"Go be with your girl," Kruso said. "I'll handle the ex-husband."

"Hey, Kruso."

She stopped and turned. "Yeah?"

"Where did you learn to climb like that?"

She smiled slowly. She really had a nice smile. "Got five kids, honey. Someone had to teach them how to climb trees."

That, he hadn't expected.

She winked and then pointed to where Kate was lying in bed, watching him. She mouthed, "Go," then shooed him with her fingers.

"Is it morning yet?" Kate asked. She sounded groggy and tired.

Walker watched Kruso walk over to an irate Ryder. It looked as if she was trying to calm him down, and Walker was tempted for half a second to go out there and talk to Slick himself. But when he looked back at Kate, she was watching him with those deep hazel eyes.

They were smoking hot for him, and there was something soft and vulnerable there too.

"Just…" He stepped up to the bed and brushed back her tangled hair.

She went to turn her head to him. "Ow," she said, and she winced and lifted her hand to touch her throat.

He leaned over her so she could look. "Don't move. What did the doctor say?"

"He cleaned the cut, gave me antibiotics for any infection. No stitches, but it hurts like hell."

He looked at the plastic brace around her wrist and went to touch it.

"It's just a bad sprain, the doctor said. He also said not to use it for a week, but how am I going to type in the computer? I have a job, and I've never missed a day. I can't just sit back—"

He leaned in and kissed her, stopping her before she could go on and on. She was so responsive. He pulled back, licking his lips. She tasted so good.

She was wearing one of his T-shirts and her gym shorts, still barefoot because he wouldn't let her get her shoes. He'd been worried she'd been hurt a lot worse than the bumps and bruises she had, so he'd lifted her up before the EMS arrived at his house and carried her to his car.

"Are you ready to go?" he asked.

She didn't say anything for a minute, but he could see the uncertainty in her eyes. "I am," she said. She started to sit up, so he slipped his hand behind and helped her up from the stretcher. "Is that Ryder?" she said as they started walking out, her hand going to the bandage covering her throat.

"Yeah," he said, watching as the doctor and Kruso

spoke with him. Whatever they said had him tearing up and then covering his eyes with his hands. Kruso put her hand on his shoulder as if trying to console him.

"Did you ever find out why his wife broke into your house and tried to kill me?" Kate asked. Walker stopped just outside the emergency room and glanced over at Ryder, who spotted him and then Kate. He looked away as if he didn't know who she was.

"His ex-wife, you mean. Apparently she and Cindy became friends. Cindy was keeping tabs on Ryder for her, told her about every date Ryder had. Every time he connected with some woman on the dating site, she'd have her email and find out who she saw. It's still a big mess. We're going to have to sort through her computer, see if there's anything tied to them that was reported. But you...I don't know what it is about you." He squeezed her to him closer, and she was watching him and then Ryder.

"How's his wife?" she asked.

"Shoulder wound. They're just cleaning her up, and she'll be off to the prison hospital."

"That's horrible," Kate said. "He's got two little kids. How screwed up is that, all because he got bored and starting messing around? Oh my God, what about Cindy? She was in my apartment."

He squeezed her to him. "Stop, would you? Boy, can you get riled up quicker than a bunch of hornets."

"I do not," she challenged. "There's just something about you that makes me lose my head."

He couldn't help leaning in and kissing her again. "Just so you know, Cindy won't be bothering you again."

"Oh, good, so you got her? That's such a relief." She

looked up and rolled her eyes, and he felt her relax against him.

He wasn't about to tell her that Cindy was dead, and they still didn't know why she'd broken into Kate's apartment and written what she had on the wall, whether that had been Ryder's ex-wife helping her or if she'd acted alone. They also had no idea why Cindy had driven her car through the front of the restaurant, but they were pretty sure it had been Andrea Connelly who'd trashed Ryder's house and slid her journal under his mattress. Walker almost thought she'd wanted to get caught. Sometimes you never got all the answers.

"Come on, let's go home," he said.

"Well, my home or your home? Where are you taking me? I mean, we haven't even had our first date," she said as he walked her out the door, and he smiled to himself, thinking he couldn't wait until then.

Turn the page for a sneak peek of
EDGE OF NIGHT the next book in the *KATE & WALKER*
series.
Available in print, audio & eBook

—"This book was hot, hot, hot!! Without fail the characters passion explodes on the page."

A. REVIEWER

—"A quick, steamy read…chock full of romance, suspense, alpha males, and strong women.

★★★★★ AHERMAN, AMAZON
REVIEWER

—"Mix love, attraction, and a mystery case and you have the recipe for a fantastic book!"

★★★★★ CAROL C., AMAZON
REVIEWER

Kate hasn't heard from Detective Walker Pruett since they shared a passionate night together. When he's assigned to investigate a robbery where she works, she knows she must protect her heart before she falls for him again…

Kate Sikes has finally met who she believes is Mr. Right, only Detective Walker Pruett isn't all about flowers and living happily ever after. In fact, after the greatest night of sex Kate's ever had, she hasn't seen Walker once.

However, she refuses to pine away for him or call him even though he invades her thoughts and her dreams— that is, until he shows up to investigate a case of robbery at the hotel where she works. Once again, Kate is left to fight Walker's charms, though she knows he can't commit and she's convinced he'll eventually break her heart.

Chapter 1

Staring off into space through the window had become Kate's pastime of late, one she wouldn't admit to anyone. She'd never been the type of woman to pine for a man, but pining was exactly what she was doing for the likes of Walker Pruett, the man who had turned a night ruined by a psychotic killer trying to end any chance Kate Sikes had of ever dating again into a night of the hottest, down and dirty best sex she'd ever had in her very young adult life. Kate was only twenty-two, and anyone would remind her she still had a lot of living and learning yet to do, but there were days she felt as if she'd lived a lifetime of bad choices, considering, when it came to men, she always picked the wrong guys.

Although Walker knew how to fuck and had driven Kate wild with a night of the kind of sex she'd never dreamed of having, he was the same as every other man she'd dated. Correction—she hadn't dated Walker, she'd fucked him, and he'd have been the first to correct her. It was sex, so she shouldn't call it anything other than what it really was.

Walker had been the detective on duty when a crazed woman had driven her car through the window of the restaurant where Kate and her date had met. The woman had headed right for her with every intention of taking her out, then had broken into her apartment to write in bright red lipstick on her wall, all because of a guy she'd met online, who, as she looked back now, hadn't been one of her better choices. No, Walker had taken her home to his place to protect her but had ended up fucking her in ways that still made her wake from a dead sleep, sweating and wanting, craving. God, how she hated him now.

It had been a month since Walker had dropped Kate off at home after her tumble down his stairs, nursing a sprained wrist, a cut to the neck, and bumps and bruises. He'd waited only long enough for her to open the door, then pulled away.

That had been the last time she saw him.

She'd expected him to call, even just to retrieve his T-shirt, which she'd worn home. It was currently washed and folded, stuffed into a drawer with her other shirts, but she pulled it out and slipped it on when she was feeling particularly lonely. Sometimes, though she'd never tell anyone, she even slept in it.

"Kate, didn't you hear me?" Keith, the front desk manager, tossed a stack of brochures on the front desk counter, behind which Kate stood in front of her computer. Her boss was a short dark-haired man with heavy brows, a round face, and a prickly attitude, and she jumped because she couldn't help feeling as if she'd been caught doing something she shouldn't have been doing. Then again, daydreaming fell under that category. Her cheeks burned.

"Yes, Keith, sorry, what do you need?" She didn't look up, instead bringing up the current check-ins and the room inventory on her screen. It was quick thinking, and she wanted to pat herself on the back, as it had kept her from landing in hot water time and again, especially as of late.

"You were staring off into space again. You need to focus on the job while you're here. Save your slacking off for when you punch out," he said in the same condescending tone he always used with her, a tone she could only put down to his need to make sure she knew her place as the assistant, not the boss. No, he was the boss, the person who could make her life easy or difficult.

She took a breath and opened her mouth to say something smart. As she looked up and across the lobby, that was when she saw him.

The panic hit her first, pulsing through her, sucking her breath out. She almost wheezed. How could she have forgotten how forbidden the man looked? He had the same short red hair and rugged shoulders, shoulders that had pinned her legs up as he rammed into her over and over, shoulders and arms she knew the feel of all too well: skin to skin in the most intimate of places.

Walker Pruett was standing not more than twenty feet from her in the lobby by the pale sofas, talking with two men, corrections cops, and damn, did he look good. She could see his badge fastened to the belt of his jeans, and his white T-shirt had her curling her fingers, as she wanted nothing more than to slide her hands over those arms, feeling the muscles flex, feeling his strength.

"Kate, are you listening to me?" Keith tapped the counter with his finger, and she felt like an idiot. At the same time, she wanted to run and hide from Walker. Of all times for Keith to be an asshole!

"Yes, Keith, I'm listening." She turned to face him, hoping he wouldn't embarrass her. He dropped another pile of brochures and papers on the counter.

"I need you to make up these kits for sales. They're short staffed today, and Shelley has calls scheduled with a group on Friday."

She couldn't believe he was passing this off on her, the grunt work he usually passed on to the front desk clerks when sales were really backed up. "Isn't this Andrea's job?" she said, reaching for the brochures and papers as the phone started to ring. She reached for it and answered. The caller wanted reservations, so she transferred it on, and Keith was still there. Maybe he was waiting for her to mess something up. As a boss, he was the worst, always focusing on what people could and would do wrong. He thrived on it. She hated that.

"Andrea is busy, and since you have all this free time to daydream and stand there looking out the window, you can put them together. It's your job when I tell you it's your job—"

"Kate."

She turned her head as Walker approached the front desk, glancing from her to Keith. She was positive her boss got off on grinding her nose into the dirt, belittling her every chance he got. Had Walker seen, heard? Of course he had. Everyone within ten feet would have picked up on Keith doing his best to make a point to Kate that he was, in fact, in charge and could make her life at work a living hell. That was a detail he had, as of late, pointed out to her on a daily basis.

"Hi, can I help you?" she said, wishing Keith would lose interest like any normal person and walk away.

Walker gave her an odd look. The way he quirked his brow, the humor or something in his expression, had her wanting to ball up her fist and ram it into his gut. So he'd fucked her and walked away, and now she was supposed to pretend…what?

She said nothing else as he tapped the counter and rested his forearm on the pale tile, his shirt doing little to hide the amazing chest she knew was waiting underneath for her touch. *Stop it!*

She squeezed her hand, fighting the unsettled feeling she knew all too well Walker could stoke inside her, making her crazy under him. She remembered what it felt like. Of course her eyes went right to that arm, seeing the shape and strength, how he had held her legs apart…

"Sir, can I help you with something?" Keith added. Kate felt her cheeks burn. She stared at her fingers, cleared her throat roughly, and tapped some keys. The screen went blank. *Shit.*

When she glanced up, Walker was looking down at her. His eyes, those amazing green eyes, were no longer smiling.

"Thanks, but I'm here to speak with Kate. Police business." His fingers tapped the badge fastened to his belt. She'd never seen him in jeans before. Maybe there wasn't a thing he didn't look good in: hot, sexy—asshole, because now Keith would be on her, thinking she'd done something illegal.

She pasted a smile to her lips, the one she reserved for guests she was anything but happy to deal with.

"Oh, I see," Keith said. "Has Kate done something I

should be aware of?" He turned from her to Walker, and, of course, he was still standing there, giving her the impression he had no plans to move any time soon.

"I don't know, has she?" Walker said in a voice that made him sound so much like a man in charge. It was something she had known all too well under him, riding him, pressed against the wall or wherever he'd wanted her.

"You know what, Keith? I've got this. I'll have all the kits put together before I go today. Is there anything else?" She glanced over to Keith, and the way he watched Walker and then looked over to her, she knew he was going to pile the questions on after, maybe make her life miserable for a while. Right now, she wanted him gone so she could give Walker directions to the door.

"Sure, don't be long. You still have another two hours before you're off."

She would have rolled her eyes, but Walker was right in front of her, and she'd had enough of both these guys. "And you will have every second of my time," she added, but the moment it was out of her mouth, she realized Keith was likely to add it to his list of her short-comings. She didn't have to look over to know, as he walked away, back into his office behind her, that he would be leaving the door open so he could hear every word spoken between her and Walker.

"I'm busy. Is there something I can help you with?" She wondered whether she could make her voice sound any more icy. She'd have loved to flip him the bird, and maybe it was the thought of doing so that added an ease to her forced smile.

"Your security footage from the cameras in the lobby

and the bar for the last seven days." He gestured toward the cameras, and his expression was one she recognized: all cop. *Asshole, not even a "How are you?" or some fucking excuse for why you did the dump and run.* Had he lost her phone number? Had he suffered a head injury and been stuck in the hospital in a coma for the past month? She had to fight to uncurl her fingers from where her nails were digging into her palms.

"I see," she said. "Well, you would need to speak with Hollis McPhail, head of security." She lifted the phone and punched in his extension, staring down at the receiver, feeling Walker's gaze burning into her.

"Security," he answered, sounding as he always did: distracted, busy, as if answering the phone was a chore.

"Hollis, it's Kate at the front desk. I have a Detective Pruett out here who says he needs to see some security footage. What would you like me to tell him?" She was hoping he'd say something like "Until he has a warrant, he can go fuck himself." She would have been more than happy to relay that message.

"Fishing for something, is he?" Hollis said. She could hear noise in the background, a pen or pencil tapping on his desk. He let out a sigh of frustration.

"What would you like me to tell him?" She looked straight at Walker, who didn't seem rattled in the least. In fact, the way he watched her and then dropped his gaze to her breasts had her wanting to reach out and slap him.

"I'll be right there. Tell him to wait."

She replaced the receiver. "Hollis will be right out to speak with you."

Now what was she supposed to do? *Awkward* was all she could think when Walker still hadn't moved but seemed to be settling in. Why wouldn't the phone ring or a guest appear so she could ignore this man who'd turned her world upside down with a night of the best sex she'd ever had? Not that she'd tell him as much. No, this smug bastard probably made a habit of bedding women and tossing them away, and she was just another notch on his bedpost. She couldn't remember if she'd actually looked at his bedpost and counted the scratches.

"You're welcome to wait over there." She gestured with the flat of her hand to the sofas in the lobby that faced the fireplace. At least then she wouldn't have to keep up the smile that was beginning to ache from how hard she was forcing it in place.

"So how have you been?"

Are you kidding me? "Great, actually. You?" What the hell was she supposed to say, that she'd spent nights sitting at home, not going out, because she'd thought he'd call? How about the number of times she'd picked up the phone just to make sure there was a dial tone? She'd had to stop herself from calling him at least thirty or forty times, because she wasn't one of those girls. She'd never, ever pine away for a guy, chase him down and leave endless messages for him to call her when it was clear he wasn't interested.

"Pretty good." He was nodding, his gaze dipping again to her breasts.

She reached for the edge of her black sports jacket and pulled it over her breasts. Even though her white blouse was decent and far from low cut, it didn't hide the size of her generous bust. No, she was proud of what she had, and she didn't skimp on bras, choosing ones that added extra lift and more cleavage. He smiled as if he knew what she was doing, but he didn't stop his ogling. The man was positively a dirty dog.

"Well, Detective Pruett who's pretty good, if you don't mind, I have work to do, so if you'd like to wait over there, I'm sure Hollis will be right out." She gestured again rather sharply, and this time she didn't smile. The fact was that she didn't want to.

He didn't move. In fact, he rested his other arm on the counter, taking in all of her as if he had every right. He was a man who wouldn't accept the brush off. He was infuriating.

"What is it with you…?"

"Detective Pruett." Hollis approached and tapped the counter before she could finish, and again Kate felt her cheeks burn. She was rattled.

"You must be Hollis," Walker said, still leaning on the counter as if he had no intention of moving. He didn't take the hand Hollis held out but instead looked and turned his head, so much the man in control, toward Kate. He winked. "Take care, Kate."

Then somehow he had his hand on Hollis's back and was walking away, far enough that she had to strain to hear. Hollis had his back to Kate, but Walker was facing her, his attention on the head of security, who was dressed in the same black jacket Kate wore, the uniform reserved for all management. He was on the overweight side, considering he spent most days glued to a desk. Whenever she saw him, he was shoveling a sandwich, donut, or whatever he had sitting on his desk beside him into his mouth.

How was it that Walker could face her from across the room and talk with Hollis, who was nodding to whatever he was saying, and Kate couldn't hear one word? She was staring at him now as he gave all his attention to Hollis.

"Kate!" Keith barked from behind her, and she jumped. "Stop daydreaming and get back to work."

When she looked back up, Hollis was walking away, and Walker was staring at her, so she picked up the brochures and papers and started sorting. When she looked up again, Walker was gone.

Coming next in The
O'Connells

THE HUNTED

When two prisoners escape and one is found dead, Marcus O'Connell finds himself being hunted—and the hunter could be someone he trusts.

One late night, Sheriff Marcus O'Connell receives a call about two escaped prisoners considered a danger to the community. A search is underway, and the warden has reason to believe the escaped convicts are headed toward Livingston. An urgent warning is issued: Shoot to kill.

Hours later, Marcus is called to a crime scene. The body of one of the escaped prisoners has been discovered deep in the woods, and the scene has already been lit up, with three prison guards standing over the body, along with the sheriff and deputy from the county over and a tracker with his dogs. A story has been neatly put together, and the group at the scene tries to send Marcus on his way.

Yet one prisoner is still missing. Marcus is told no investigation is necessary, that he should sign off on the case and walk away. But nothing adds up. The problem is that dead men can't talk, and Marcus can't shake the feeling that the story he's being told is a coverup for something far more sinister.

The Hunted

CHAPTER 1

The sound of crickets punctuated the quiet neighborhood. Darkness had settled in, but Marcus needed a minute, as he leaned against the large porch beam, before he could lock up for the night and feel that all was okay in his part of the world. He lifted his hand in a wave to his brother Owen and his wife, Tessa, as they drove away in her small compact. Again, he took in the neighbors' houses. Next door, the lights were off and all seemed quiet.

Ryan and Jenny were already inside their house across the road, and the outside light was now off. Marcus waited for that feeling he got every night before locking up, an assurance that it would be okay for him to lay his head down and go to sleep. He counted heads, making sure everyone was okay, listening to the sounds inside his house, the fussing of Cameron, who was doing his nightly protest against going to sleep.

The screen door squeaked open behind him, and Marcus turned to see his dad step out, wearing blue jeans and a black t-shirt. He heard his mom and Reine talking inside. His dad nodded to him and headed over.

"Your mom is finishing up in the kitchen with Reine and Eva," Raymond said. "That boy of yours is just like you. You always fought your mom and argued every night about how you weren't tired, but a second later you'd be out cold. You didn't know how to stop."

Marcus turned to look back at the street. He was still trying to understand his dad. He leaned against the post on the porch, breathing in the warm summer night. The smell told him tomorrow would be another hot day.

"You were rather quiet tonight," Raymond said. "Everything okay?"

What was he supposed to say? This feeling had come out of nowhere. He couldn't remember ever having felt so unsettled, and he didn't have a clue what had caused it—family, life, something else?

"Just one of those days, you know," Marcus said, unable to find words to explain it.

His dad only nodded. It wasn't lost on Marcus that his dad had been forced to stick around Livingston because his mom had refused to leave her children and grandkids. His dad had a way of seeing everything. Marcus had figured that much out, but a stranger wouldn't have been able to tell, as Raymond never let his gaze linger too long.

Now he did, narrowing his eyes, peering out into the darkness. The stars were out, and a few streetlights were on. "Always the sheriff, looking out to make sure everyone is tucked in, safe," he said. "Expecting trouble?"

Marcus looked over to his dad. Inside, the house phone was ringing, and a second later, it was answered.

"You know something I don't?" he said. The sarcasm dripped.

His dad only shrugged. Marcus heard footsteps and pushed away from the post just as the screen door squeaked again, and Reine stepped out, her dark hair pulled back, wearing a peach sundress, barefoot.

"Marcus, it's for you," she said. "It's Therese." She held out the cordless phone.

Marcus didn't look over to his dad, who he knew was watching him in the way only Raymond O'Connell could. Marcus took the portable phone. "Thanks, Reine," he said, then waited as she walked back in the house. He put the phone to his ear, glancing only once to his dad, knowing his deputy called only if there was something he needed to handle. "What's up, Therese?"

"Sorry to call so late, Sheriff, but I have a message from the warden from Montana State. Two prisoners have escaped, and all he said was that they could be headed this way. I was about to call him back…" There was static on the line. His deputy was cutting in and out, as if she were driving.

"Hey, Therese, you're cutting out. You said two prisoners escaped from Montana State?" He was already walking back into the house and taking the stairs two at a time. Upstairs, Charlotte was reading to his son, whom he thought he heard jumping on his bed. Marcus was in his bedroom now, yanking open the closet door and opening the gun safe to retrieve his .357 SIG.

"Sorry, Sheriff," Therese said. "I'm about twenty minutes away, and the cell service is like shit out here. Picked up the message on the way. All it said was that two prisoners escaped. The warden is…"

"Kellogg," Marcus cut in, fastening the holstered

gun to the waistband of his jeans. As he closed up the gun safe, he pictured a man he'd met only a few times.

"I missed that part of the message," Therese said. "I'll give him a call and let you know what he says."

Marcus glanced to the open door. His wife now stood in the doorway. "No, Therese, I've got it," he said. "I'll have Charlotte check the message, and I'll give the warden a call."

She said nothing, and he noted her hesitation.

"Anything else?" he said, realizing it had come out rather short.

"No, that was all," Therese said. "You sure, Sheriff? I don't mind making the call. It may be nothing."

"Or it may be a lot," he said. "No, I've got this one." Then he hung up and held the phone out to Charlotte, taking in her wide eyes.

"What's going on, Marcus?"

He reached for his badge. "Prison break or something along those lines. Therese just called, said the warden at Montana State left a message. Two prisoners. I need you to get his number and play that message for me."

She was already nodding and dialing the office. Something about his wife handling phones and dispatching again settled him in ways he couldn't explain. She scribbled down the number on a pad of paper on the dresser just as his two-year-old son came running in, all smiles, appearing nowhere near ready to go to sleep.

Marcus reached for him and gave him a toss in the air, then held him and kissed his cheek. "Hey, you. Giving your mom a hard time? You're supposed to be asleep."

"Not tired."

"Yeah, well, you will be soon. Go get a book and get in bed."

"Here, Marcus, the number," Charlotte said. "The message is kind of garbled, but yes, it's something about two prisoners escaping."

He put Cameron down after kissing him again and reached for the paper and the phone, shaking his head over his rambunctious son.

Charlotte shook her head. "He's going to be the end of me. You know he argues every night about how he isn't tired?" She pulled her arms over her faded green t-shirt, her dark hair pulled up in a ponytail. "You're heading out, aren't you?"

"Yeah, after I call the warden," he said. "I don't like this."

There it was, that smile of hers he loved. She leaned in the doorway, glancing once over her shoulder down the hall to where their son's bedroom was as he dialed the phone.

"Montana State, warden's office." The voice was muffled, and Marcus had to really listen past the rough twang.

"This is Sheriff O'Connell, from Livingston. Is the warden there? I've got a message from him about a prison escape."

He heard a rustle on the other end, then a clunk. Evidently, whoever had answered barely knew how to use a phone. "Yeah, yeah," the person said, then yelled out, "Warden! Call for you from that Sheriff O'Connell."

Marcus reached for his wallet and stuffed it in his back pocket, then reached for his duty belt. Charlotte didn't look away, gesturing for an explanation, but Marcus only shook his head. There was another rustle on the phone.

"Sheriff? Warden Kellogg here." The man had a deep voice. "Afraid two prisoners escaped. Was discovered only a short time ago by one of the guards. We're in lockdown now. Just finished a count and are interrogating some prisoners. We know two got out for sure, but how, we have no idea. They likely had help from inside. I suspect they could be headed your way. These men are dangerous, both of them. I've already contacted state officials, as well, along with the other sheriffs in the area. An order has already been issued: Shoot to kill."

Marcus angled his head, looking right at Charlotte. He wasn't sure he'd heard the warden correctly. "You can't be serious," he said. "Who authorized that order? With all due respect, Warden, capturing the prisoners is the first priority."

"Sheriff O'Connell, these prisoners are a danger to the community," the warden said. "They will slit your throat and kill you without a second thought. If you want to dance around them and be the nice guy, do it on your own time and not at the detriment of the good people of Montana. You see them, you shoot them, because these two will do anything and everything to avoid capture. Killing, maiming, looting, burning. You want the details of what they'd do to your wife and sisters, everyone in your family, everyone you care about? If you want to argue with me about bringing them in alive, you can do it, but I don't want these two getting anywhere near innocent people. I've already reached out to Judge Harris, and photos of the prisoners have been sent to you."

Marcus didn't have a clue who these two prisoners were or what they'd done, but that sick feeling was back in his stomach with the image of the horror the warden had painted. Damn, what kind of evil had the two men done?

On the other end, the warden was talking to someone else. Then he addressed Marcus again. "Anything else, Sheriff? If not, I suggest you get your ass out there and start looking. Stan has faxed over the photos, and emails have gone out statewide."

Something about Warden Kellogg had always unsettled Marcus, but he couldn't put his finger on what it was. "Yeah, you said they could be headed my way. Why is that? They have family, friends, contacts here? I need all that information."

"Everything about both prisoners has been sent to you. One has a girlfriend, I understand, outside Livingston, and a brother up toward Billings. If that's all, Sheriff, I've got a fucking mess to handle here. You have any questions, get in touch with Sheriff Lester up in Stillwater County. He's got more on them, and he's been on this since word went out. And, Sheriff O'Connell? A word of advice. I understand you may want to give these men a second chance, but sometimes we're all better off if a criminal is six feet under. You understand?"

Yeah, he understood, but a knot twisted in his stomach as he looked over to his wife. He wondered if this explained the sick feeling he had or the cold sweat that had broken out up his spine. "Understood," he said.

"I'll start looking." Then he hung up and tossed the phone on the bed.

"What is it, Marcus?"

Marcus counted the extra clips in his duty belt, then walked over to his wife and ran his hand over her shoulder. "Warden says the prisoners had help from the inside to get out. Says they're dangerous. Photos have been faxed and emailed. Can you access those? I'm going to ask Mom and Dad to stay until I get back," he said. It was just a feeling he had, the need to keep his family together. "See if you can pull up the prisoners' files, too. Warden said they've been sent. I want to know everything about them: who they are, what they did, and exactly how dangerous they are."

He hurried down the stairs, and Charlotte was right behind him. Raymond was back in the house, and he could hear his mom, Reine, and Eva in the kitchen. Marcus stepped off the bottom step, and Charlotte moved around him into the living room, over to the small desk where her laptop was.

"What's going on?" Raymond said as Marcus reached for his sheriff's jacket and lifted it from the hook.

"Marcus, I just sent the photos and files to your phone," Charlotte called out.

Marcus pulled his iPhone from his coat pocket and turned to his dad. "Can you and Mom stay?"

Raymond didn't seem surprised. He only nodded and said, "Yeah, of course. You worried about something?"

Marcus pulled out the keys to his cruiser. "Two prisoners have escaped and could be headed this way. Warden says they're dangerous, so much so that he wants us to shoot first and ask questions later, so I don't want to leave Charlotte, Reine, and the kids alone."

He knew his dad understood. "Yeah, you got it," he said. "You be careful."

Marcus thumbed through his phone and pulled up the photos his wife had sent. One was dark skinned, the other lighter, both with dark hair and brown eyes, the same bugged-out mugshot expressions. Their names were Rafe Jackson and Holter Donnelly. "Charlotte, send these to Harold and Ryan, too," he called out over his shoulder as he opened the door, and his dad was right behind him, holding the inside screen. "Charlotte has the photos," Marcus told him. "Take a good look."

Raymond nodded. "I'll call Ryan and Owen," he said.

Marcus lingered just outside. He didn't know what to say to his dad. Out of anyone, he knew Raymond had a handle on this. "Thanks," he finally said, then started down the steps. He heard the door close behind him and the lock flick closed.

He dialed his cell phone, walking straight for his cruiser and climbing in. As he tossed his duty belt and coat on the passenger seat, the phone rang once, twice…

"Okay, what did you forget?" Suzanne answered. He thought he heard Arnie fussing in the background.

"Put Harold on," he said, shoving his cell phone in the mount on the dash. He started the car.

"No can do," Suzanne said. "He's in the shower. What is it?"

There she went, playing interference. He knew she was still pissed at him because he wouldn't let her play cop in his county.

"You tell Harold to get the hell out of the shower and call me back," he said. "There was a prison break. This is serious shit, Suzanne. Charlotte just sent him the photos and files. I need him to dig into it and then meet me at the office. I'm not messing around. Have him call me. Can you do that?"

She was quiet for a second. "Don't take my head off, Marcus. Yeah, I'll tell him. Hey, big brother?" She always seemed to need to have the last word.

"What?" he said as he backed the cruiser out, ready to get off the phone. He flicked on the headlights and gave the vehicle gas, looking out into the darkness, knowing he'd be taking a second and third look at anyone he saw that night, scrutinizing who they were and what they were doing.

"Watch your back," she said.

He felt a smile tug at the corners of his lips. "Always do," he said. "Now have Harold call me."

Marcus ended the call before his sister could add one more thing. As he rounded the corner, feeling his own angst, he drove slower than usual and took a good, long look at the few pickups parked along the street, scanning for anyone out walking. There was only a couple with a dog.

This was going to be a really long night.

CHAPTER 2

Marcus stood outside the station in the dark, looking right and then left, tracking the headlights of a car as it went by. He heard the distant laughter of a few teens skateboarding just up the block. He was getting a sense for who was out, doing what, and where.

He pulled out his key and shoved it in the lock, then pulled open the door. The hallway was dark, but he didn't flick on the lights as he strode down it, his footsteps echoing. The lights were on inside the county sheriff's office, and he thought he heard voices.

When he opened the inner door, Therese was there, her dark hair pulled back, wearing blue jeans and a gray t-shirt. Colby, the junior deputy, was there too, which Marcus hadn't expected. He wasn't in uniform but instead wore a jean jacket over what he thought was a red t-shirt with a Confederate flag. Both were standing by Charlotte's desk and the fax machine, holding papers.

"Sheriff, the photos and files of the two prisoners came in," Therese said. She held one for Rafe Jackson, the same one he'd already seen. "Colby just got off the phone with Sheriff Lester, who has all his men out looking."

Marcus dragged his gaze over to a quiet Colby. "And?" he said, taking in the young deputy's round face and eyes that were more brown than blue. Colby was lanky and tall, but Marcus still had a few inches on him. He hated this twenty-questions shit, and for a second, he didn't think Colby was going to divulge anything.

"He said not to worry about coming out," Colby said. "He has his men doing a grid search with the dogs, and he told me to pass along that you can stay close to home. They've got this."

Marcus just stared at Colby, then dragged his gaze to Therese. He couldn't shake the feeling that there had been a lot of discussion before he walked through the door.

The door opened behind him, and he expected Harold but glanced over his shoulder to see Suzanne, wearing the same blue jeans and bulky blue shirt under a faded old jean jacket, her long brown hair hiked high in a ponytail. She closed the door behind her.

"Where is Harold?" Marcus said. "Please tell me you're not bringing the baby, too."

Suzanne made a face only she could. "I'll have you know Arnie is at home, fast asleep, and so is my husband. I left him a note."

For a moment, he just stared at his sister, wanting to snap. She'd always been the hardest one to read. "Suzanne, this isn't the time for you to pull this crap. You understand there's been a prison escape? Call Harold. You go home." He knew it had come out rather sharply, but he just turned back to Therese and Colby, who were watching the siblings with wariness. His frustration ramped up as he gestured at Colby. "And what were you about to tell me, Colby? You don't get to talk to another sheriff as if you're running things here. Sheriff Lester has no jurisdiction to tell you to pass along a message like that, as if I shouldn't worry my pretty little head."

"No, Sheriff, sorry, that wasn't what I meant," Colby said. "Or rather, it wasn't what Sheriff Lester meant. I'm sure he was just trying to be helpful, is all."

Now, why didn't Marcus believe that? "So that's it? That was all he said to you? You call him, or did he call here? Because I'm pretty sure my cell phone didn't ring."

Therese was now looking at Colby, and Marcus was starting to sense something else was going on.

Colby looked down to Charlotte's desk and the papers there. "I was here first, and there was a message from the sheriff. I called him, thinking I could get a head start on things before you got here, is all. He told me they're already on it and there's no need for you, that they have all the manpower they need. That's all, Sheriff. He was neck deep, and I could hear the dogs in the background. We didn't talk long."

Marcus glanced back to his sister, who had her arms crossed, watching Colby. She shot Marcus a significant look, and he heard himself let out a weary groan under his breath. He pulled out his cell phone. "I spoke with the warden," he said, "and he figures there's a girlfriend here in Livingston and a brother outside Billings. See what you can find out." He flicked his gaze to Therese, then over to Colby. "Both of you, start digging. What came through on these two?" He took in the message from his wife, a PDF, and tapped it open to see the mugshots of Jackson and Donnelly again, along with their arrest dates, prison records, and next of kin.

"We have a list of misdemeanors for both, nuisance charges, as well as trouble in prison," Therese said, holding out a paper with the same notes that had been on his phone. "Career criminals, by the looks of it. Verbal threats, assault involving a police officer, criminal mischief, unpaid fines…"

Marcus reached for the paper, because Therese had to be missing something, but it was truly just a bunch of petty misdemeanor charges. A pain in the ass, for sure, but not dangerous. The public defender had been the same for both of them, George Wallace, someone he'd never heard of.

"Therese, call the warden back and find out where the rest of the file is," Marcus said. "And call this public defender, Wallace, and find out from him what I'm missing about his clients. We were given an urgent warning, shoot to kill, which is not something I take lightly, and what I'm looking at here doesn't warrant that. I want to know what they haven't told me about how dangerous these two men are. I have a town full of people who have no clue about these prisoners on the loose. If anything, I need an alert put out to everyone in town to be on the lookout. You both got it?"

"Yes, Sheriff, absolutely," Therese said, already on her way to her desk. Colby was still holding some papers, which Marcus snatched from his hands, but they were just a duplicate of the misdemeanor charges, as if someone had just kept faxing the first page.

"Colby, you tell me everything that was said between you and Sheriff Lester?" Marcus said.

Colby looked up at him with wide eyes. "He was just rushed, impatient, is all. Sheriff, he said not to worry, that he's got it."

Marcus glanced back to his sister, who only shrugged and widened her eyes. She thought she was being coy, but he knew her better. He dragged his gaze back to Colby. "Yeah, well, I doubt that. He's got nothing in my part of the county. Go and give Therese a hand." He turned to his sister. "You, come with me."

Marcus headed for his office, hearing Therese on the phone already, wishing Harold were there. He waited as his sister walked into his office behind him, and he flicked on the light and closed the door behind her, holding the knob, taking a second. He walked over to his desk and dumped the papers on it.

"I know what you're going to say, Marcus."

"Oh, I highly doubt that," he said. Everything in his sister's face, her passion, her life, reminded him so much of the little girl who had tried to tag along on whatever he and Ryan had been up to as kids. They'd spent so much time ditching her, and it seemed she was still trying to find a way to sneak in, only now they were grown-ups, and she wasn't scared of anything.

"You don't have to be so nasty," she said. "Besides, you've got Therese and Colby out there, making calls for you. You really should get notice out to the public. You don't have to give details of what they've done, but you need their photos out there so people in the surrounding area know to be on the lookout and not open their doors for a stranger. We don't want someone to take the trash out and find one of these two hiding in their yard. People need to know to lock their doors tonight, Marcus, and maybe keep that shotgun in easy reach."

He just stared at his sister, knowing she was right, but it was only because she was messing with him and interfering in his business, police business, that he wasn't already all over it.

"Don't worry, Marcus," she said as she pulled open the door. "I can handle this for you, and then I promise you I'll call Harold."

He just stared at her. The phone was ringing from Charlotte's desk, and he heard Colby answer it. "Fine," he said. "Handle it. Get the notice out to local TV stations and cell phones, and then you call your husband and go home."

Whomever Colby was talking to, he was now writing something down. "Yes, I'll let the sheriff know," he said. "He'll be right out there." Then he hung up. Marcus had just stepped back around his desk when Colby lifted the notepad and called out to him, "Sheriff, they found them! One's dead, just past Miller's Field. They need you out there to sign off. I can tag along."

Marcus stared at Colby with a sinking feeling. Maybe it wouldn't be such a long night after all. "No, it's fine," he said. "You go on home. I've got this." Then he looked back to his sister, who was giving him that wide-eyed look. He shook his head and said, "You may as well come with me."

There it was, a smile. For a second, he wondered whether she'd do a victory dance.

"Don't get too excited," he said. "Just making sure you don't turn this office upside down."

"Now, don't be nasty, Marcus," Suzanne said, thumping his chest with her fist as she walked past him and pulled open the door.

Marcus glanced back over to Therese, who was now

off the phone. "You too, Therese, head on home. I'll call you if there's anything else," he said.

Then he was out the door behind his sister, letting out a heavy sigh as he took in the paper he held. He knew well the location, a secluded spot in his county. His sister should have been home with her baby, yet there she was, sticking her nose in his crime scene.

"Well, are you coming, Marcus?" Suzanne called from the door and gestured impatiently.

"After this, you go home," he told her. "Better yet, I'll drop you off."

She only angled her head, then gave it a shake and fell in beside him as they walked out to his cruiser. Harold's Kia was parked right beside him.

"You didn't tell Harold, did you?" he said, though it wasn't a question.

Her hand was on the passenger door. Her mouth tightened, and she shrugged. "He really did fall asleep. I left him a note."

He shut his eyes as Suzanne opened the passenger door and climbed in. Yeah, he was going to have to have a word with his deputy about dealing with his sister. He slid behind the wheel and started the car. "When we get out there, Suzanne, I want you to stay out of the way."

"Whatever you say, Marcus," was all she said, and he knew she didn't mean it. Damn, at times, he really did have a ton of sympathy for Harold.

"Lorhainne Eckhart is one of my go to authors when I want a guaranteed good book. So many twists and turns, but also so much love and such a strong sense of family."

(LORA W., REVIEWER)

New York Times & USA Today bestseller Lorhainne Eckhart is best known for writing Raw Relatable Real Romance where "Morals and family are running themes." As one fan calls her, she is the "Queen of the family saga." (aherman) writing "the ups and downs of what goes on within a family but also with some suspense, angst and of course a bit of romance thrown in for good measure." Follow Lorhainne on Bookbub to receive alerts on New Releases and Sales and join her mailing list at LorhainneEckhart.com for her Monday Blog, all book news, giveaways and FREE reads. With over 120 books, audiobooks, and multiple series published and available at all, retailers now translated into six languages. She is a multiple recipient of the Readers' Favorite Award for Suspense and Romance, and lives in the Pacific Northwest on an island, is the mother of three, her oldest has autism and she is an advocate for never giving up on your dreams.

"Lorhainne Eckhart has this uncanny way of just hitting the spot every time with her books."

(CAROLINE L., REVIEWER)

The O'Connells: *The O'Connells of Livingston, Montana are not your typical family. A riveting collection of stories surrounding the ups and downs of what goes on within a family but also with some suspense, angst and of course a bit of romance thrown in for good measure. "I thought I loved the Friessens, but I absolutely adore the O'Connell's. Each and every book has different genres of stories, but the one thing in common is how she is able to wrap it around the family, which is the heart of each story." (C. Logue)*

The Friessens: *An emotional big family*

romance series, the Friessen family siblings find their relationships tested, lay their hearts on the line, and discover lasting love! "Lorhainne Eckhart is one of my go to authors when I want a guaranteed good book. So many twists and turns, but also so much love and such a strong sense of family." (Lora W., Reviewer)

The Parker Sisters: *The Parker Sisters are a close-knit family, and like any other family they have their ups and downs. Eckhart has crafted another intense family drama… "The character development is outstanding, and the emotional investment is high…" (Aherman, Reviewer)*

The McCabe Brothers: *Join the five McCabe siblings on their journeys to the dark and dangerous side of love! An intense, exhilarating collection of romantic thrillers you won't want to miss. — "Eckhart has a new series that is definitely worth the read. The queen of the family saga started this series with a spin-off of her wildly successful Friessen series." From a Readers' Favorite award—winning author and "queen of the family saga" (Aherman)*

Billy Jo McCabe Mystery: *The social worker and the cop, an unlikely couple drawn together on a small, secluded Pacific Northwest island where nothing is as it* *seems. Protecting the innocent comes at a cost, and what seems to be a sleepy, quiet town is anything but.*

Lorhainne loves to hear from her readers! You can connect with me at:
www.LorhainneEckhart.com
lorhainneeckhart.le@gmail.com

facebook.com/AuthorLorhainneEckhart

twitter.com/LEckhart

instagram.com/lorhainneeckhart

bookbub.com/profile/lorhainne-eckhart

pinterest.com/lorhainneeckhart

In the Silence
In the Charm
Unexpected Consequences
It Was Always You
The First Time I Saw You
Welcome to My Arms
Welcome to Boston
I'll Always Love You
Ground Rules
A Reason to Breathe
You Are My Everything
Anything For You
The Homecoming
Stay Away From My Daughter
The Bad Boy
A Place of Our Own
The Visitor
All About Devon
Long Past Dawn
How to Heal a Heart
Keep Me In Your Heart

The O'Connells
The Neighbor
The Third Call
The Secret Husband
The Quiet Day
The Commitment
The Missing Father
The Hometown Hero
Justice
The Family Secret
The Fallen O'Connell

The Return of the O'Connells
And The She Was Gone
The Stalker
The O'Connell Family Christmas
The Girl Next Door
Broken Promises
The Gatekeeper
The Hunted

The McCabe Brothers
Don't Stop Me (Vic)
Don't Catch Me (Chase)
Don't Run From Me (Aaron)
Don't Hide From Me (Luc)
Don't Leave Me (Claudia)
Out of Time

A Billy Jo McCabe Mystery
Nothing As it Seems
Hiding in Plain Sight
The Cold Case
The Trap
Above the Law
The Stranger at the Door
The Children
The Last Stand
The Charity
The Sacrifice

The Street Fighter
Finding Home

The Wilde Brothers

The One (Joe and Margaret)
The Honeymoon, A Wilde Brothers Short
Friendly Fire (Logan and Julia)
Not Quite Married, A Wilde Brothers Short
A Matter of Trust (Ben and Carrie)
The Reckoning, A Wilde Brothers Christmas
Traded (Jake)
Unforgiven (Samuel)
The Holiday Bride

Married in Montana
His Promise
Love's Promise
A Promise of Forever

The Parker Sisters
Thrill of the Chase
The Dating Game
Play Hard to Get
What We Can't Have
Go Your Own Way
A June Wedding

Kate & Walker
One Night
Edge of Night
Last Night

Walk the Right Road Series
The Choice
Lost and Found
Merkaba
Bounty

Blown Away: The Final Chapter
He Came Back

The Saved Series
Saved
Vanished
Captured

Single Titles
Loving Christine